MY NAME IS AMERICA

The Journal of Jedediah Barstow

An Emigrant on the Oregon Trail

BY ELLEN LEVINE

SCHOLASTIC INC.

New York   Toronto   London   Auckland   Sydney
Mexico City   New Delhi   Hong Kong   Buenos Aires

Overland
1845

May 12

It's almost two weeks now, and today is the first day I opened this book. It was Mama's journal. I been carrying it since Mr. Fenster gave it to me. Only thing he found in the river, he said, besides me. It's all dried out now, but there's a big watermark like a long peninsula coming out from the binding. Fat at the beginning and skinnier toward the edge of the page. They never found Mama, Pa, and Sally.

Ole Missus Cavendish has brought a coffin with her. She is afraid the wolves or the Indians will dig her up if she passes on the journey, so she wants to be six feet down and in her box. She's hoping, of course, she won't need it before we get to Oregon. They couldn't have used her box for Pa, Mama, and Sally even if they had found them, 'cause there was three of them.

Later

Mama's hand flows smooth but not so even. She always wrote real fast. She used to laugh when Pa said it wasn't lady-like. "Never no mind, so long as you can read it, Josiah. It's the words that count." I can hear her saying it, too.

The story starts on the inside cover. We're all there:

Sarah Rachel Gibbs. Married Josiah Barstow 14th day of January, 1831.
Jedediah Barstow, born 16th day of December, 1831.
Sally Martha Barstow, born 20th day of May, 1836.

Jedediah, that's me.

Mama said she was going to keep the story of our journey to Oregon so that "the grandchildren, and great grandchildren and all the way unto the seventh generation" would know what this Grand Adventure was like. I guess I am the one to keep the account now.

I wonder if she would want me to write "Josiah, Sarah, and Sally Martha Barstow, passed the 28th day of April, 1845"?

I hate Oregon.

May 14

I don't feel like talking to anyone. Mr. Perkins grunts a
loud "Hmmph!" whenever he sees me, like I'm some
pesky rodent he's trying to chase away. Ole Missus
Cavendish was walking by the other day and heard him.
"Jasper Perkins, you are an exasperatin' grouch!" From
now on he is "Mr. Grouch," so far as I am concerned.

The problem is, I don't like it when Missus Cavendish
says something, either. It's always, "So how are you,
Jedediah Barstow?" She peers at me through those glasses
that always slip down her nose. It's right strange how she
is shorter than me, but her head tilts *down* when she's
looking *up* at me. Anyways, she's a nice lady, but sometimes I can't help it, I just walk off. Mama would say
that's plain rude, but who wants to talk about losing your
family? Since Missus Cavendish has got her coffin with
her, she probably never stops thinking about death. I
mean, every time I think about it, I feel like I'm choking.
I know Mama would tell me to "stop avoiding."

May 15

I can hear Mama's voice almost like she was looking over my shoulder. All right, Mama, no more avoiding. This here's what happened:

It was mid-day when we got to that muddy, miserable Kaw River. The wind was picking up a little, but still the sky was clear. There was a long line at the ferry. It wasn't really much of a ferry. Just a log raft with some bracings at the front end and sides. The ferrymen locked the wagon wheels with long poles through them and then looped ropes through side hooks on the wagons and down to the edges of the logs. There was thirty-six wagons in the company, and it was taking so long, it'd be well past dark before we all got over. So some wagons started to ford. The current didn't seem so bad, and Pa got in that line.

Jacob Fenster got his own wagon across first. Then he rode his horse into the creek and searched for firm spots, marking them with poles. The first wagons pulled down the bank and into the water, following Mr. Fenster's train markings. I think about six crossed, when out of nowhere a streak of lightning split the sky open. I'd been watching the wagons so hard I hadn't really noticed it was darkening, but Pa should have. The thunder boom was louder than a cannon. The rains came in thick sheets, so's you couldn't see more than six inches in front of you. A blue-black darkness, with these sudden shafts of blinding light.

We'd been next in line, and just when the sky opened, Pa pulled into the creek. Our two yoke was so skittery, their tails swatted wildly back and forth. Pa was in the water trying to lead the team. I was gonna be on the other side, but Mama said she needed me inside the wagon. We tied down as much as we could and then we gripped the side ropes ourselves. I leaned against Sally to keep her from sliding. She was too scared to cry. Eyes wide open, breathing fast, hanging on to the rope real tight. With every blaze of lightning I could see her knuckles, white like chalk. Mine must have been, too. We was lurching across by inches, heaving side to side. We pitched forward so sharply I lost my grip and banged up against Mama. She grabbed my arm and pulled me to the rope. I crawled back over to Sally. But just when it seemed to steady out a bit, we must have hit a sandbar. The river tore through the wagon and I got washed out.

I was underwater, being whipped around. I couldn't see anything but swirling sand and a dark shadow off to my left. I think it was the wagon tongue, but when I reached for it I couldn't get near enough. There was nothing but the sand water. I was gulping in bucketloads.

Something dark brushed up against me, and when I reached up, I got a handful of hair. Horsetail! I didn't know if I could hang on.

Next I knew I was lying on the bank, my face partly in the mud, and Jacob Fenster was pounding my back. I don't know for how long. I woke up wrapped in blankets inside Mr. Fenster's wagon, and he was sitting looking at me. He handed me a cup of tea.

And that's how I come to be an orphan.

May 18

I feel lighter. This writing is like the yeast Mama used to make bread rise. Pa always said Mama's bread "rose and was mighty . . . Mighty light, that is!" he would add, 'cause Mama always worried about it being too heavy.

Later

If you're telling a story, start at the beginning, Mama always said. Well, I did, 'cause it started with the drownings. After that, I stayed with Jacob Fenster for about a week. I don't remember much of those days. I know it was blazing sun most of the time, but all I saw were the shadows on the ground. "Expecting to find your future on the road?" Mr. Fenster kept asking me. But that didn't make me look up. I just kept staring at the solid ground. I could hear people whispering, "Poor boy! Poor boy!" whenever they saw me.

The only thing I really remember is getting in that fight with Jack Simpson. I bloodied his miserable nose and he deserved it, calling me "Orphy boy" and making a chant of it:

> "Orphy boy is all alone
> Staying with the Jew!
> Two of 'em is all alone
> Ain't with me and you!"

Over and over he said it. Some of the others, too. The only one standing real quiet was a girl I heard someone call Lucy.

I ran at him. Took him and me by surprise 'cause he's bigger than me and probably would have got me bad if he'd swung first. The other kids stood around hollerin' until Ned Appleton broke it up. He's older. I was mad he pulled me off Jack.

Anyways, that night I looked at Jacob Fenster closely. He seemed like everybody, except he did talk a little

9

strange. But so did some other people. Still, maybe there *was* something different about being a Jew. Why else would people talk about them? Then I remembered the meeting I went to with Pa in Independence the night before all the wagons pulled out. They took a vote whether or not to stop traveling and lay by on the Sabbath. There was some hot talk. In the end I think Pa turned it all. He said only God would judge if we were bad Christians, and we should stop looking nasty at each other.

I wasn't sure what that had to do with traveling on the Sabbath. When I asked him later, he told me the story of a famous preacher from Cincinnati who said he wouldn't jump off an ocean liner in the middle of the sea just 'cause it was traveling on the Sabbath.

At the meeting everybody voted except Mr. Fenster. When I asked Pa why, he said, "It's not his Sabbath, so he's leaving it to us." I never thought more on it at the time. But after the fight with Jack Simpson, I been wondering.

One night when we was eating supper, I asked Mr. Fenster what it means being a Jew. He got that same look Pa would get when he was thinking hard. But he kept on chewing. I thought he'd never say a word.

Finally he said, "When you look for meaning, you search your own way. Some people pray to the God of their fathers when they ponder on the miracle of a blade of grass. Some think on it by themselves without God. If we're praying men, you and I might call God by a different name. But we're both praying just the same."

Then he left the wagon. I got to thinking. Grass was what the cows ate. Didn't look like no miracle to me. It was enough everybody was looking on me as different. I didn't need to be staying with another being who stood out. And so I left Jacob Fenster's wagon. I know he saved me, but I left anyways. Mama would say it was cowardly not to even say good-bye, but Mama's not here.

That night I stayed around the main campfire real late. The grown-ups was all in their wagons or tents, but the older boys and girls was still about. I didn't know where I'd lay out my blanket, but it weren't going to be by Jacob Fenster's wagon. I hung to the back of the circle, behind Ned Appleton and that girl he's been mooning over. He's real nice when he's showing me things, but dumb when he looks at that girl that way.

It started to drizzle, and I crawled under the closest wagon and lay down my oil cloth and blanket between the wheels. I don't even remember falling asleep.

Someone kicked me and yelled, "Outa there, boy!" Woke me real quick. My luck to crawl under Mr. Henshaw's wagon. He's about as sour as Mr. Grouch. It was just after four in the morning, 'cause he got me up to help bring in the cattle. All the men were getting ready for the roundup. I remember Pa saying there was about 700 animals in the company, between the oxen and the cows and the horses. The horses, of course, was tethered right outside the corral, but the cattle was out there in the grasses, fattening themselves up.

I'd always stayed by our wagon when Pa went out, 'cause Mama needed me to start reloading, getting everything ready to go. Same thing I did with Mr. Fenster. But I wanted to go on the roundup like some of the other boys, driving all them oxen in to be yoked up and getting the loose cattle in a herd, ready for the drive. So I was real glad when Mr. Henshaw woke me. It was just too bad it was Mr. Henshaw.

We didn't get finished for over an hour. Didn't matter how many oxen and cows you had. Everybody worked everybody's animals. When we come back to the wagon, Missus Henshaw was leaning over the kettle with her back to us. I forgot and almost shouted, "Mama!" She turned and smiled at us. Caught me up for a minute. But the smell of the food was real powerful. Even the same old bacon, bread, and beans was maybe the most delicious breakfast I ever had. Still, I kept thinking about Mama.

* * *

Anyways, Mr. Henshaw near spat at me, "You can stay, boy, but you'll work for your keep. And you know I mean work!" He turned that mean squint of his on me. I nodded yes, but that weren't good enough. "Speak up, damn it, boy!" he hollered.

"Yes, sir. I'll stay, sir."

I don't know why I said it. I know I could have found some other wagon what needed help. Missus Henshaw had a tiny smile when she poured me a cup of coffee. I think she was glad I was going to be with them. And from the back of the wagon Rebekkah cried, "Stay! Stay!" I guess she wanted me, too.

So that's how I come to be with Mr. and Missus Henshaw and Bekky, who's seven years old.

May 20

Been raining so hard for the past two days, the wagons can't move for all the mud. It's just stopped, but still too muddy to travel. Lots of folks was drying out things around a big fire in the middle of the corral. Jason Welch said, "Crossing the Kaw where we lost the Barstows was the first real flick of the elephant's tail. This here's another."

Mr. Grouch muttered, "If you have enemies, persuade

'em to make a land journey to Oregon!" The men all laughed, but Mr. Richardson looked kinda funny at his missus.

Only thing I saw at the Kaw was Pa taking us into those black waters. When I asked Missus Henshaw about elephants, she said there's folks think this journey's so risky, it's like meeting an angry elephant. You either face it down or you turn back.

It picked up raining again, and we corralled in a steady drizzle. Captain Osborne's pilot scout picked the site, but it didn't seem to me one place was much different from the next. It was all mud. The Captain sat on his horse like he always does and sent one wagon to the left and one to the right, arching out to make the big circle. It always puts me in mind of Mama reading the story of Noah to Sally and me. Two by two, until they made the corral. The difference is our animals go outside. It's only us inside. And of course there is nothing dry about this Ark.

Once the corral is made up, we have to unyoke all the oxen and drive them and the cows out to graze. It usually takes at least an hour. It was even longer last night 'cause they was spooked by all the storming.

May 21

Still too much mud. Mr. Henshaw's rear wheels got stuck real bad. I was helping Missus Henshaw, when he grabbed my arm and pulled me over. "Damn it, boy. Why ain't you knowin' when I need you?" Maybe if he ever said my name I'd come sharper. But all he does is holler, "Boy! Git over here!" or "Where you been, boy?"

He told me to cut some long grasses and lay them on the ground in front of the wheels. Once the wheels were unstuck and rolling, they'd turn onto the grass and slowly come up out of the mud. Mr. Simpson, who is Jack's father, Mr. Bennett, Mr. Morrison, and one of the Taler twins was pushing and pulling while I layed down the grasses. Mr. Henshaw was whipping the oxen up front. The Talers had brought over their team to add to Mr. Henshaw's. It was mid-day before the wagon was moving again. By then the sun was out and things was beginning to dry up. Mr. Simpson's real nice. Hard to ponder on Jack being a part of him.

Looks to me like a wheel bolt is loose by the back right axle, but my lips is sealed. Last time I tried to tell Mr. Henshaw something, he near twisted my arm off. It was when I said how Pa fixed the tongue hinge when it come loose.

"Don't like it? Why you staying, boy? Why you staying?" Keep hearing that in my head, and I have no answer. After we was freed up of the mud, Missus Henshaw was real nice at dinner and gave me an extra pinch of sugar in my tea.

May 23

We lost two days with all the mud. But today it's as clear as if the sky never knew the word rain. I was glad to hear the Captain holler, "Roll out!" this morning. Been missing that call.

We nooned above the bank of the Little Blue River. Missus Henshaw traded Missus Sedlow sugar for some eggs and then made a fine dinner out of them. I put the ones she didn't use into the flour barrel, spacing them out so each one had its own "bed," as Bekky called it. She kept laughing, seeing my arm get all white and the flour dusting up in my hair.

Later

Chased after some wild turkeys to catch one for Missus Henshaw, but lost them all in the tall grass, like they was swallowed up in a sea. When I come back, Missus Henshaw and Missus Sedlow was talking about setting camp here even though it's only a little past noon.

"There's enough sun to do the washing," Missus Sedlow said. And Missus Henshaw agreed. "Captain Osborne has to understand after all that mud everything needs a powerful scrubbing." I guess the Captain agreed, 'cause in a short while they got fires going down by the riverbank, and kettles boiling over with water. The piles of unwashed linens is almost as tall as me.

I'm wearing one of Mr. Henshaw's shirts. He didn't look happy about it, but Missus Henshaw said she was gonna be doing a wash, and my shirt was a part of that. I think she's stitching me up a new one, which will be a good thing.

Bekky asked me why people called the river "Lil Blue" when it's a lot bigger than she is and everyone calls her Lil. And besides, she said, it weren't so blue. I don't recall asking so many questions when I was seven. She's a little like Sally that way. She's a real chatterbox with her Mama, and now me. But she's different from Sally 'cause she locks up real tight when her pa's around. Hardly ever says a word in front of him, but then nobody says much around Mr. Henshaw 'cause he snaps at you like a pestered turtle.

Night-time

It's a bright moon, and when I roll up a blanket, I can lean real comfortable against the wagon wheel. Mr. Henshaw's snoring. Don't imagine Missus Henshaw's getting much of a sleep. Heard someone call her "Sarah" today. Funny, she's got Mama's name.

May 24

We'll be by the Platte River tonight they say. Captain Osborne calls it the Great Platte Road. The men elected him twice to lead the company. The first time out of Independence was sort of a test to see if the company thought he'd be good. They called it the "preliminary election." Then just before we got to the Kaw River, they elected him again. So I guess they think he knows enough. I myself think he should've stopped Pa from crossing, since Pa didn't have sense enough to stop himself. Makes me hot to think on it.

Bekky wanted to know how a river can be a road. I never know what she'll ask next. Told her we'd have to wait and see.

May 25

We're at the Platte and it looks like a wide muddy stripe running up through the grasses. There's also lots of sand in the water, and it glints in the sun. "It's a confusion," that's what Sally would have said — how the river can be muddy and sparkle-y at the same time. The confusion to me is how one day we're soaking in mud, and the very next we're parched as dry as a paper cinder. Back when I was with him, Mr. Fenster gave me a hat for all this sun, since mine went down the river with everything else.

We been climbing up and down some rough bluffs to reach the Platte. My feet is toughening real quick, which is good since there'll be more holes than leather in my boots before too long.

Later

The road goes some of the time along the bluffs and some of the time down on the river bottoms, which can be sixty feet down and real wide. Mr. Henshaw hollers a lot when we're camped on the bluffs 'cause then we have to go down the hill and all the way across the bottom to get to the water. Don't know why he complains, though.

Regular as the sun coming up and going down, *he* hollers, but sends *me*.

May 26

For the first time since I left him, I was in nodding distance of Jacob Fenster. He was standing by Captain Osborne's wagon, waiting on the rest of the men for the council meeting. He was right pleasant but I didn't say a thing. I have been keeping clear of him, but Missus Henshaw sent me with a message for the mister who was also waiting on the council meeting.

Night-time

The Henshaws are asleep, and he's snoring again. I have to write down about this noon's council meeting, for it was about me! The Richardsons are going back. "The first turnarounds," Missus Henshaw calls them. Maybe she wishes she was going back, too.

Mr. Richardson's got a real bad cough and sometimes fever. Some of the ladies think he might pass if they don't go home. They was all talking at the campfire tonight that it's the bad air at the bottoms. He should lay up in the sun on the bluffs. That'd burn the ague out of him. Mr. Grouch said, "It weren't the fever . . ." Then he snorted. "It were the elephant!" Anyways, they're going back.

Seems maybe that elephant tail is flickin' near me. Someone at the meeting said, "Why don't the orphan Barstow boy go with them?" Missus Simpson told Missus Henshaw who told me that Jacob Fenster objected, "The boy's old enough to have his own mind." And so they come to ask me. It was Hiram Littleton who come. And that's probably why I'm still here. If it'd been Mr. Fenster, I'd have told him to mind his own mind. And if it'd been Mr. Henshaw, who knows what I might have said? But Mr. Littleton's real soft-spoken. To everybody, including his boy, Amos. Picks out his words as careful as he does his tools. I seen him carve wedges for wagon wheels that have shrunk in all this dryness. He takes care, not like some who whittle away fast like they're real angry at the wood. That's Mr. Henshaw, who I think is angry at most things, me in particular.

Anyways, it was Mr. Littleton who said to me I had some real important pondering to do and not much time to do it in. Just until tomorrow morning, in fact. I could go with the Richardsons or stay with the company. So I should think real hard, he said. "The question is," he said, "are you looking back to the States, or ahead to tomorrow?" That was it. Then he left.

I climbed up the bluff to the grasses. Just me and the sun. Uncle James and Aunt Caroline were back home. But they didn't have children and never paid much mind to us when we visited with them, 'cept, of course, to tell us to quiet down. That's what was back there.

Ahead? Tomorrow? Can't think what that means. If I think about what's happened, I'm ready to turn back. I feel real angry at Pa. If he hadn't . . . Never mind. I'll worry more on it later.

May 27: Early before the morning bell

Have to be careful about this writing. Mr. Henshaw saw me last night when he come out of the tent for some water. "What you writing, boy?" and grabbed it away. It made me so mad I hollered back, "That's mine! You give it to me!" All the fussin' woke up Missus Henshaw. It was the first time I heard her raise her voice, and even then it was low. "That's a piece of the boy's memory, Asa. Now you give it back to him." I think he was so surprised at her laying down an order, he did it.

*   *   *

I'm thinking on what I should do. I remember Pa talking about what a Grand Adventure we was going on. Mama at first wasn't so sure. After supper Pa would read out loud the newspaper articles about "Oregon Fever," but Mama would laugh and call them tall tales. One night I went with Pa to the meeting where a speaker was telling about the Willamette Valley in Oregon. "You want to know what it's like?" he asked. "I'll tell you the real story":

Under the cedar groves, and there's more than you can count in Oregon, the pigs run around already roasted with a knife and fork sticking out of their sides! All you have to do is slice off a chunk whenever you're hungry!

The men all laughed, but I thought it sounded miraculous. When I told Mama, she said the only miracle was that he was convincing all these otherwise smart men to pack up everything and leave for something they knew nothing about.

Then one night sometime in late February, when even the cows was moaning in the barn from the cold, Mama caught the fever. We'd been sitting by the fire, Mama and Pa doing I don't remember what, but not talking. I know I was working on my sums. Suddenly, as if in the middle of a conversation, Mama says, "If the land's half as rich as they say, it would be wonderful to have a long growing season and easier winters." When I looked up, Pa was smiling. And that's how we come to be going to the Willamette Valley in Oregon.

Damn Pa! If we hadn't come, we'd still be a family! Maybe I'll be struck down for the blasphemy. But the stars are still up there and the moon is moving regular. I can hear Mama's voice saying what she said to me and Sally every night: "Don't go to bed with regrets and you won't have them when you get up."

Later

When I was bringing back the dishes from rinsing, Missus Henshaw was packing the wagon. The mister was over by the Captain's with the other men, fixin' the day's planning. "Don't be getting too upset by Mr. Henshaw, Jedediah. He lost everything when the crop failed last year." She closed the lid of the grub box, and that's all she said.

Mr. Littleton come by, walking with Amos. I told him I was staying.

May 28

They all keep talking about the Pawnees. This is their territory, but I haven't seen any yet. We passed a Kaw village sometime back, but it was right after Pa, Mama, and Sally were lost, and so I weren't at full attention, as Pa would've said. I heard the Captain telling Mr. Littleton that the Kaws was supposed to be a thieving lot, but that they certainly was honorable with us. I missed all that.

But maybe the Pawnees are more like the stories. The Taler twins have told some fiercesome ones about them. Around a campfire last Saturday night they sat there spinning ghost stories and then near frightened us half to death, talking about Pawnee ambushes and murders. Mr. Grouch snorted, "Tall tales, tall tales! Taller than the Tower of London!" Mr. Grouch does not believe anything. And I don't know how tall the Tower of London is. But the Talers' stories have lodged in my mind.

The Talers really are twins, Micah and Jeremiah. Wonder if they got into storytelling because of their name.

May 29

The weather's a real confusion: bright sun, soft wind, and then a sudden ambush of hailstones the size of lemons. The hail tore right through the Henshaws' tent last night. Mr. Henshaw is furious that I didn't get hit bad 'cause I was blanketing under the wagon. They will all sleep inside the wagon till Missus Henshaw sews up the tent. I don't expect it to be too peaceful tonight.

May 30

Nooned by a prairie dog town. Mr. Littleton said it must be near 300 acres. These critters are a bit bigger than the gray squirrels at home, and no wonder they call them dogs. They have this real squeaky bark whenever you get near one of their houses. There's always one of them sitting by their front door, like someone on the porch, chattering away to anyone passing by. Mr. Littleton says Jacob Fenster says there's more of them here than people in New York City.

That's when I said something real dumb about New York being "Jewtown," so I guessed Mr. Fenster would know. It was something I'd heard Mr. Henshaw mutter. My first mistake. Mr. Littleton put down the harness he was working on and looked at me, real disappointed. "You don't judge a man by the God he prays to, Jedediah Barstow."

Most times when someone calls me by my full name, I know it's fiercely serious. I think I must have turned the color of Pa's flannel shirt, my face was so hot. Then I aggravated it by saying, "He said he lived in New York City one time, didn't he?"

Mr. Littleton looked at me. He spoke so calmly that if you didn't listen to the words, you wouldn't know he was mighty angry: "I think you've got some thinking and apologizing to do, Jedediah Barstow. And if Jacob Fenster's going to understand your apology, you will have to tell him what you said."

That was two whole times he said my full name.

After supper Missus Henshaw gave me the new shirt she'd stitched up for me. It fit perfectly, and I thanked her, but I didn't much feel like I should be getting any presents.

May 31: Mid-afternoon

There they were this noon! Maybe eighty Pawnees altogether. Ned Appleton told me they're on their way back from their big spring hunt. They've got piles of antelope and buffalo skins. I was standing with him, looking at all those skins, when Missus Cavendish and Abigail Pringle come by. Seems those two are kinfolk.

Abigail was telling how the Indians jerk much of the meat to put it by for later times. First they cut it up in thin strips, and then dry it real slow over fires. It keeps a long while that way, she says. Ned thinks she's real smart. You can tell the way he looks at her. I guess she knows this stuff 'cause her Pa was once an army scout.

We was late starting up 'cause the Pawnee chief and some of his men come right up to our wagons. They made known they wanted some things from us 'cause we was traveling through their land, but Captain Osborne turned it into a trade, and that's how I got my first taste of buffalo. It's pretty juicy and a lot strong, but that's kind of nice after all the bacon we been having. The Indians stayed around and ate with the rest of us before they left. No murdering nor massacre-ing, just trading and eating.

We've started to jerk the meat. Missus Henshaw was slicing all afternoon. She's hung the strips on ropes along the sides of the wagons. We don't have the time, she said, to dry the meat over a fire. The hot sun will do the job. I guess you learn about these things when you need to.

June 1

I've not talked to Mr. Littleton these last days. I been too busy helping with the cattle. We've had to wade them across to some of the islands in the river for the grass, 'cause there's been nothing on the bottoms for them to eat. Buffalo have grazed it all off. So I don't have time like I usually do to visit with him. Besides, I know he's waiting on me, and I don't have anything to tell him. I haven't talked to Jacob Fenster yet.

Later

It's the Sabbath, and Reverend Mr. Turnbow was preaching after supper. Me and Charlie Smothers was listening. Charlie's my age, even the same birthday month. He's traveling with his uncle and aunt, the Welches. His folks passed of the cholera a year and a half ago, and he's been living with kin ever since.

Anyways, we was watching the Reverend real intently 'cause of the way his hands fly around when he shouts about the sin of breaking the Sabbath and the punishment for sinners. He's been traveling with us all along, but maybe his sin gets washed out 'cause he's instructing us on ours. Sometimes when he's holding forth, he smacks someone passing by. Of course he don't mean it, but it's a sight worth waiting for.

Most people nod to him as they pass, but few has the time to stop doing their business. There's too much fixing and cleaning and packing and unpacking the wagons. Missus Henshaw says she means no disrespect, but she's comfortable doing her own praying in her tent.

After about half an hour of stern talk at us few listeners, the Reverend dropped to his knees and prayed to God real loud, "Remove, dear Lord, the wild beasts and savage men from our pathways!"

"I sure hope the Lord don't hear all that prayer!" Charlie whispered to me. "I want to see more Indians."

"And a grizzly!" I whispered back. I really wanted to see the big bear with the long nails.

June 2

The rear right wheel finally come off. I knew something would happen with that loose bolt. First thing in the morning, too. Mr. Henshaw was out on a hunt, so Missus Henshaw was walking one side of the team and me on the other. A hawk went down after something not far from us. Beat those wings fast on the way up with a prairie dog squawking in its beak. Happened real fast, but upset one of the team, and you only need one for them all to get spooked. They pulled the wagon sudden and sharp to the left. The next thing the wheel's off and wobbling into the grass. Like a lightning crack, the axle snapped.

I wasn't thinking about Bekky when I didn't tell Mr. Henshaw about the bolt. But she was riding in the wagon when it happened. A chest toppled over and banged her upside her head. Left a bump over her left eye, but she is not hurt bad. Missus Henshaw was shaken, though, 'cause if Bekky had been closer to the front, she might have been knocked out of the wagon. When Mr. Henshaw come back, he looked at Bekky and then complained to Missus Henshaw that they had too many chests they were carrying.

There's a boy been lying inside his family wagon for the last eight days, 'cause he fell under the wagon wheels. He was riding the tongue as we was going down a small ravine. The front wheels dropped into a rut, and the boy was thrown off. Wheels broke both his legs and two ribs. The team got spooked by his shrieking and sped up, tumbling the wagon straight down the gully. In the end, even more got broken than just him.

Captain said it was a piece of luck that he only broke his legs. At first it didn't seem so to me. But then Missus Cavendish was telling that in other companys there's been boys and girls dead of falling under the wheels.

When she was waiting in Independence for us to pull out, she saw one family that had turned around and come back when their boy died early on. He was sitting in front, whipping at the team, when the wagon went over some rough ground, and he fell under. They waited, not wanting to cut off his leg, hoping he'd mend, but they waited too long. Mortification set in, and they couldn't save him.

It's a fiercesome thought that it might have been Bekky. And it would have been my fault for not saying about the bolt.

Mr. Littleton come by to see about Bekky. Makes me uncomfortable when he looks at me with those light eyes of his that sees clear through to the back of your head. Then Mr. Fenster brought over a special tea for her to drink. Says it will make her feel less ache-y. Missus Henshaw was real grateful, sitting them down and bringing out a little cake she'd made the other day. I nodded when Mr. Fenster smiled at me, and left the wagon real quick.

We're stuck here till the wheel's fixed. Pa was always good about checking things like that. Back home when he took the wagon out on long trips, and nothing were as long as this, he'd walk around it, fingering the wheel bolts, checking everything. I've never seen Mr. Henshaw do anything like that. "Waste of time," he'd likely say. But I make a promise. I will say something next time I see something. It's a promise I'm making for ~~Sally~~ Bekky.

Night-time

It's Mr. Henshaw I should be avoiding, not Hiram Littleton and Jacob Fenster. He was at me again today. "Hey, boy! Git up off your bum and git that basket filled for the missus!" She never likes it when he yells at me, but I'm not her son. This time, though, she did say something. She said I always do get her the buffalo chips when she needs them, and that she'll take care of it. He needn't worry on it.

I think he just wanted to yell at me. Don't know which is worse, Mr. Henshaw's holler, Mr. Littleton's stare, or Mr. Fenster being nice.

June 3

Layed by today 'cause of the ox foot disease, which Captain Osborne calls the "Foot Evil." Mr. Littleton's got the good tools, so he was called to do the cutting. Mr. Fenster, knowing about medicines, was also there. The Taler twins and Mr. Bogart was helping out, too. Don't know whose ox it was they cut first, but I was watching hard. Lot of the boys were there, including Jack Simpson, but just like me he was too intent to start a fight.

And this here is why. First they dug a trench and then they rolled the ox over into it, so it's lying on its back with its legs in the air. Then they staked some ropes across it. It let out a mighty bellowing, but big as it was it couldn't move. Mr. Littleton chiseled off the cracked part of the hoof. You could see the dry prickly grass that had got caught in the cracks. Must have hurt that poor creature bad to step on it. That foot was swelled up the size of a small melon. Then Mr. Littleton sharpened up one of his carving knives, put the blade in the fire, and cut away the bad flesh. When it was cleaned up, they poured hot water and then hot tar on the hoof. The bellowing was something fierce.

Don't know who was hollering louder, the ox or Mr. Henshaw who was squawking mad. One of his cows had been limping so bad, she tripped, broke her leg, and he had to put her down. He was cussin' so loud, it took Captain Osborne to quiet him down and remind him he'd have a few beef dinners out of it. Matter of fact, the ox they was operating on got quiet before Mr. Henshaw did.

June 4

All those scrapped and tarred oxen were walking today. Never mind the hollering, it really does work! Puts me in mind of being an animal doctor. Some of the oxen even have buffalo skin boots wrapped around their feet, the hair side facing in. I'll be needing that real soon, what with my boots more holes than boot. I think I'll pass on the tarring, though.

June 5

Captain Osborne sent a group of ten men out to get us some buffalo meat. Most of them are not good shots, being plowmen like Pa back in the States. So they probably won't be back before dark.

Mid-day

There's lots of islands in the river. And as treeless as it is on the bluffs, it's a forest in the middle of the Platte, at least on the islands we been by so far. Waded over to the biggest one at noon for some wood for Missus Henshaw's fire. The water was warm and never above my knees, which is the way I like it.

June 6

I was right. Half past ten last night the hunters returned. Some of us was around the central fire waiting. They was bragging about how many they killed. Mr. Littleton got heated. "God forgive us for the waste and save us from the ignorance!" They jumped on him, saying it was fine sport for the men, and we needed the meat.

"You're just shooting and shooting with no mind for anything but trophy horns!" he said real sharp. "Don't take much to feed all of us for many days." It got extra heated when he argued to limit the kill. Somebody took a swing at him and had to be restrained by the Captain. Then a bunch of them turned their backs on him and stood paying him no mind. It was almost enough to make me agree with Mr. Littleton. Excepting, of course, I want to go out on a hunt. But Mr. Littleton weren't finished. He said we was making it hard for the Indians who depended on the buffalo for nearly everything. That was going a bit far, the Captain said. I thought so, too.

June 7

Missus Henshaw was real tired this morning. She and the other ladies stayed up almost through the night dressing the buffaloes the men brought back. We was real lucky. They left a buffalo stomach near last night's campfire, and this morning it was all swelled up tight like a ball. We got two teams kicking and butting that stomach ball around. First I just watched, 'cause I got there late. Mr. Henshaw had me rubbing grease on the axles. I got over to the game just before Amos Littleton twisted his ankle. He's a little one, but he runs real fast and kicks hard. When he fell, I got in the game. My first run I butted the stomach ball into Jack Simpson's side. It give me some pleasure it was him blocking our side.

June 8: Mid-day

I was back of the wagon and pretended I didn't hear Mr. Henshaw calling me when we stopped for dinner. "Leave him be," I heard Missus Henshaw say. I went up from the river and way out into the prairie grass. Just wanted to lie down in the sun. Laying there was like floating on a huge waving sea of grass and under a gigantic sea of sky. So blue that sky, when you layed down and stared up, it cheered your insides. For the first time since the Kaw, I felt real quiet and still. Peaceful. I must have layed there for close up to an hour, 'cause I thought I heard the Captain's bell way faraway, signifying roll-out.

I jumped up fast. All around was prairie flowers and tall grass swaying and rustling in grass talk, but saying nothing about direction. With the sun overhead, there was no easy telling east or west, north or south. The river was hidden. I'd climbed a bank some sixty feet up from where the river had carved its way through, but where *was* the river? I kept hearing a voice in my head saying, That's what you get for feeling happy, dumb boy! I was breathing real fast, getting dizzy and seeing spots from staring so hard. Was this a flick of the tail? . . .

Then I remembered something Jacob Fenster said one day. He said the buffalo always know the way to the river. "Look at their tracks. Straight like you layed them out with a ruler." There it was, the grid just like he said. Each row was maybe fifteen inches apart and some four inches deep. Rows on rows of straight trail lines, all heading toward the river. I started running. Pretty soon I could see the edge of the bluff, and then across the bottoms to the river. And there was the wagon train! Moving slowly like a lazy snake in the hot sun.

Night-time

Been pondering. Jacob Fenster rescued me again.

June 9: Real early

Didn't sleep so good. Went to Jacob Fenster's wagon before roundup call. I started telling him while we walked out of the corral that I was sorry for saying dumb things. He let me kinda sputter on, and then real solemn he said, "I appreciate your apology, Jedediah. I do truly appreciate it." Mr. Henshaw started hollerin' for me, and Mr. Fenster waved me off. Feel light like one of Mama's rolls!

Mid-day

We're just above the forks. Here's where the north and south branches of the Platte separate out. At the council meeting this morning Captain Osborne was saying he thought we should take the lower ford over the south fork 'cause it would save us some days. I been hanging around when the council meets, but of course I don't say a word. A couple of the men wanted the middle ford, which is some twenty-two miles away, saying it was an easier crossing, but the Captain made the final decision.

The river is about a quarter of a mile wide, I heard them say, and maybe up to three feet deep. But no storming. We've been lucky that way. We've crossed over all size of creeks. Some days it seems like we do nothing but wade in and out of streams. Don't like crossing over anything above my knees, though. I'm not afraid. I just don't like it.

Mr. Littleton checks on me whenever we come to a ford. Mr. Fenster does, too. I wish they wouldn't.

Later

When Mr. Fenster laid out the pole trail through the river, it put me in mind of something bad. Looking at the pole heights, you could see we'd have to hit some sinkholes where it was real deep. The animals could swim, but the wagon beds would get flooded. There was no storm, but you'd likely get all wet. I was thinking I don't like this at all.

Captain and the men figured a way to keep most things dry. First we had to empty out the wagon bed of everything. Mr. Henshaw didn't stop complaining. "Sarah, why we need this?" He tossed her little chest on the ground real hard. When he flung the rocker down, the left runner snapped in two. "Well, that ain't coming back on this wagon!" he said cheerfully. Missus Henshaw untied the knitted pillow from the chair and gave it to me to put in the trunk. His hollering made me so mad I didn't think too much on the crossing itself. At least for a while.

As soon as the wagons was emptied, the wagon box was lifted up off the bolster, and blocks was shoved underneath. When the box was lowered back down, it was riding about six inches higher. Then we tarred up the cracks between the boards. Captain come by telling folks to lighten up the loads. "Take only what you truly need." Everybody was leaving things, but with a lot less yelling than Mr. Henshaw. The riverbank was filled. Chests, chairs, extra tools, and one real big mirror in a carved frame that was never going to see Oregon.

After we reloaded whatever we was taking, the wagon

boxes was cinched down tight to keep them from floating off when we hit the river. We was all packed up again, but I just didn't want to go into that river. As our wagon rolled down the bank to the water's edge, I told Mr. Henshaw I was staying back to help ready some of the other wagons. He shrugged. Probably couldn't think fast enough about something for me to do.

Keep seeing Mama and Sally hanging onto the ropes. But I don't like not wanting to cross. So when the Taler twins' wagon finally was ready, I asked if I could go with them. It was somewhere around nine o'clock and dark with not much of a moon. I sat inside making sure the ropes didn't come loose. Micah was in the water on the left side steering the oxen, and Jeremiah on the right. It was dark enough, so even if they'd been in the wagon they wouldn't have seen how tight I was hanging onto the ropes.

It took the whole afternoon and well into the night before everybody was crossed over.

June 10

Told Mr. Littleton this morning that I talked with Mr. Fenster. He looked up, nodded, and went back to work.

He was mending a broken axle. Mr. Littleton gets called whenever there's the need. It's the buffalo ruts on the road, he says. Keeps the wagons bouncing for miles. Even with the grasses poking up through the holes in my boots, I'm happy to be walking. The bouncing is enough to make butter out of milk without anybody doing the churning! It's true 'cause I saw the milk can Missus Henshaw strapped to the wagon side. By suppertime she fished out a ball of butter at least an inch thick. And there was lots more little pieces. Imagine what that churning does to your insides.

I took Amos walking with me to help out Mr. Littleton, 'cause he had a lot of work to do, and Amos was too full of energy to stay in one place. He was hopping around like a grasshopper discovering a whole new field just waiting to be chewed. When I told him about the bouncing butter and the churning inside his own stomach, he just laughed and jumped a little higher.

June 11

By the end of this trip, everybody is going to have a bouncing story. Lucy Sedlow told me about when she was layed up with a real bad cold and had to stay wrapped up in blankets inside the wagon for five days.

With all the rain making things worse, they kept the drawstrings closed tight, and she said it was the worst seasickness she ever felt. She's been on a steamboat on the Mississippi during a rainstorm, so I guess she knows something about that kind of sickness. She said this was the worst. She was trapped in the small space of the wagon, and throwed up near everything she ate. She made me swear never to tell.

I told her about Mr. Littleton's heavy eye on me. She said he was right about Mr. Fenster. She even said she told Jack Simpson he was just plain dumb for what he says about Mr. Fenster being a Jew. I wonder if that's why he stopped chanting that "Orphy Boy" thing. But even though me and Jack was wrong, still, she agrees, a heavy eye is a heavy thing to bear. So she was glad for me it was over.

Lucy and me really became friends when a whole group of us was gathering up buffalo chips, me for Missus Henshaw, Lucy for her mama, same like everyone else. The boys was tossing them like saucers. I'd just flung one at Jack Simpson and he, back at me, when another bounced off my back. When I turned around, it was Lucy. She ducked right smart when I tossed one back at her, and so I missed. Then we all heard the noon-end bell, and raced to gather the chips up. Didn't collect near as many as we'd tossed.

Lucy and I got to talking when we was walking back. We was laughing real hard about something. Just as we got to the Henshaw wagon, she was saying, "Did you ever think, Jed Barstow, back in the States you'd make a friend while collecting buffalo chips?" She's the first person since Mama, Pa, and Sally to call me Jed.

Bekky was standing outside the wagon, and "chips" was all she had to hear. Yelled out she wanted one right then and there. Seems back home Missus Henshaw used to make real thin-sliced roasted potatoes they called chips. "Ooh, they was so DEE-cious!" she cried.

I almost choked, but Lucy stayed right calm and straight out told Bekky what buffalo chips was. "You know when you go to the outhouse?" she said. "Well, the whole prairie's the buffaloes' outhouse." Bekky's eyes got bigger and bigger, but Lucy kept on talking. "You see, these buffalo patties dry out real nice and then you can collect them when you don't have any wood, and make a fine fire with them. Watch what your mama does tonight and you'll see." Lucy was so solemn, there was nothing for Bekky to do but nod solemnly also.

And that is how Lucy Sedlow and me come to be friends. Talking about buffalo chips and outhouses.

June 12

We've been walking up and down bluffs for days, and down into the sandy-bottom ravines. Nothing is as big an irritation as the spikey grass coming up through boot holes. My feet bottoms have these sore spots that look like a pox has been flourishing. Sinking up and down in the sandy soil is a sight better than walking on the grass. It don't hurt, but you do work up a mighty appetite.

Ned Appleton says the emigrant who is not hungry is a sick emigrant. Amen to that. The dried, fried flour patties, which is what we're chomping down on most of the time, and the same old beans and bacon is getting fairly tiresome. I eat it all anyways, but I'm still hungry. Ned also says the man who eats the most breakfast, eats the most sand. He's right there, too.

The only good thing about the sandy soil is I been walking barefoot in it. Sparing what little leather is left, is the way I'm thinking on it.

June 13

Layed by today to rest the animals. It appears most of us two-leggeds need the rest as well. Cleaning and fixing is happening all over. There's oxen getting foot treatments, dusty clothes getting clean treatments, axles getting Mr. Littleton treatments, and Missus Simpson is giving out hair treatments. She cornered me, and the next thing I know I was sitting atop her barrel while she snapped her scissors over my ears and behind my neck. Felt like I was getting a scalping like the Taler twins tell about. All the while she was talking to me like I was Jack's friend. I didn't say a word. Jack was by the wagon having just been sheared clean by his mama. The more she talked about us being friends, the more he kicked at the ground, till she told him he was creating a storm and we didn't need any more dust than we already got. I sneaked a look at him, and grinned. I know we were thinking the same thing: mothers. Always making like everybody is good friends.

Started me thinking about Mama. She always did Pa's hair, and mine and Sally's, too. Just like Missus Simpson. I think Mama would have liked Missus Simpson.

Later

The twins not only tell tales, but they make music, too. At the central campfire tonight Micah was singing and playing harmonica and Jeremiah was fiddling next to him. Missus Cavendish was having a fine old time harmonizing with Ned and Abigail. She was even elbowing Mr. Grouch to join in. "Now, Jasper Perkins, lighten up your soul and sing! I know you can!" Most he could get himself to do was hum. A bunch of the young girls was dancing in circles. Lucy was leading Bekky and some of the other little ones in a line dance. Then Ned and Abby started the grown-ups twirling around in twosomes.

Missus Henshaw was looking right interested, but Mr. Henshaw said he wasn't no fancy footer. He talks loud enough so it wasn't surprising Mr. Fenster heard him. Most of us did. Anyways, Mr. Fenster came over. "Might I dance with the missus?" he said to Mr. Henshaw while he was nodding at Missus Henshaw. "Don't trouble me none," was all the answer he got. And that's how I got to see Missus Henshaw smile for the first time in many weeks.

June 14

Right now Missus Henshaw's cooking up supper, but round mid-day we didn't know if we was ever going to be eating again!

Samuel Hall, Captain Osborne's pilot, had been ahead of the wagons some miles, looking for tonight's campsite. I was fixing the harness ropes, when I noticed Missus Henshaw's milk can was banging on the wagon side even though the wagon wasn't moving.

"STAMPEDE! STAMPEDE!" Mr. Hall was hollering so loud his voice was cracking. He rode up in a cloud of dust, whupping the side of his horse like there was a sizzling fire back of his tail.

I ran over to Captain Osborne's wagon where the councilmen was gathering. Somebody shouted, "Must be a thousand of 'em!" The Captain grabbed hold of the Taler twins even before Mr. Hall got off his horse and sent them to the hill on the right side of the camp. "Look for the biggest bull and start shooting in front of him. Don't stop till they turn! You understand what I'm saying to you? DON'T STOP TILL THEY TURN!" The twins raced off to get their firearms. Four others joined them.

Mr. Fenster, Mr. Littleton, and Mr. Simpson was dispatched to start a line of fires the other side of the ridge in front of the camp. Another group ran to get spades to tear up the grass behind the fire line and dig a trench between that line and the ridge. That way the fire would have a hard time spreading up the ridge and down to our camp. Mr. Simpson sent Jack to pick up the powder bag from his wagon and me to get some cotton rags. I was too excited right then to be scared. Thinking on it now, that was just plain dumb. Mr. Littleton said a big bull can weigh as much as 2,000 pounds. And that's what was bearing down on us!

Crouching in front of the ridge, all we could see was a

black sea surging toward us, shooting up huge dust clouds. The soil was flying behind us from the group digging up the ground and spading out the trench. The pounding underfoot was something fierce. The men could only motion to each other, 'cause the thundering of the hooves drowned out any talk. Jack gave his father the powder, and I handed him a cotton rag. Mr. Simpson rubbed the rag in the powder and shot it out of his musket. He did this several times. The flaming rags lit up the grasses in front of us, and the fire spread down the line. We leapt back of the trench and raced up the ridge.

I couldn't hear the Talers shooting, the roar was so loud, but I could see all the men up there was loading and shooting, loading and shooting. Captain Osborne stood on top of the ridge with Samuel Hall. I got up there in time to hear him say quite calmly, "If these mammoths come over the ridge, they'll crush the wagons in a matter of minutes. Are you a praying man, Mr. Hall?"

That set me thinking on a most powerful plea. But "Dear God, make 'em turn!" was all I come up with. I kept repeating the words over and over. "Make 'em turn! Dear God, make 'em turn! Make 'em turn!" It flashed through my mind, "This is the whole elephant!"

If Mr. Hall wasn't a praying man before, the next sight surely would have made him one. Like the parting of the

Red Sea, the sea of mammoths split in two right in front of the fire line. One half surged to the left around the camp, the other half to the right, circling completely around us. Our company of wagons never looked so tiny. Then the two streams rejoined and plunged in a united mass across the river to the plains beyond.

June 15

Made about sixteen miles today. It was a good travel day even though Mr. Henshaw was in a foul mind much of the time 'cause it's our turn to be in back. We been rotating which wagons is up front and which behind. Only fair way, the Captain says, so that nobody eats more dust than anybody else. Mr. Henshaw doesn't see it that way. Far as he's concerned, anybody else eating dust is better than him.

Missus Henshaw and Bekky was at Missus Simpson's wagon. Missus Henshaw said she was working on repairing a piece of quilt. But I think she needed a piece of quiet.

So I got it all. And today it wasn't just the dust. "Muskeetows!" That's what was provoking Mr. Henshaw the most. "Drat muskeetows! EEEEvil muskeetows!" He scratched out the word like it was a nail going across an

A-B-C board. I was almost getting to tolerate muskee-tows for all the trouble they was giving him. I would never let him know, but I admit they *was* fierce at the bottoms. They come at you like it was real personal. And they head for a place out of reach. The more Mr. Henshaw swatted, the fiercer they swarmed. When Missus Henshaw come back to make dinner at mid-day, he was hollering, "How can I eat when I been et alive, dang blast it!" I had enough of an appetite, but I was glad we was moving on.

Later

We corralled by a fine spring with lots of grass for the cattle and wood for the fires. Mr. Grouch was saying it were God's joke that we have lots of wood just when we are drowning in buffalo chips. Not much difference to me, since I'm the one gathering whatever there is. Can't toss the wood like plate saucers, though.

Forgot to write down Mr. Fenster's cure for muskeetow itching. Chew on some plantain leaves, and rub the glob on real good. Worked fine on my legs and neck, but there's fierce itching on my left hand won't go away.

June 16

Lucy says there's all manner of wonders in this land. She was talking about the Courthouse, which we passed early this morning. Leastwise that's what the Captain calls it. In the slanting sun, it truly does look like a mighty building, but I have never seen a real courthouse, so I can't say of my own. We can see Chimney Rock up ahead, shooting straight up to the sky. Be there mid-day I expect.

Some of the older boys walked over to the Courthouse 'cause it appeared just a stone's throw away. They didn't get back before dark. It was more like seven miles off. Real hard to tell distance. Either you can't see for the hills, or the prairie's flat out like a gigantic plate, and no telling where the rim is.

Anyways, they climbed up one side where there was holes cut in the rock face. They said they had a grand view of Chimney Rock. There was a lot of talk about the Chimney back in the States. Right before your eyes, people said, stands the tallest chimney you've ever seen, marking the desert like a signpost! It's not really a desert here, but back in Missouri I guess they didn't know that.

Mid-day

We nooned right up near the Chimney! A couple of us boys took off as soon as we stopped. In little over an hour we were at the base. Me and Charlie Smothers and Jack Simpson scrambled up. Climbers before us had carved their names in the rock. I had the knife Pa gave me for the trip. The blade edge is honed smooth, and the knife has a carved walnut handle that looks real smart sitting up out of the leather sheath it come in. Anyways, I started to make my marking, when Charlie said, "Bet you can't get any higher!" Next thing it was me climbing over Jack, climbing over Charlie, and round again. We was panting and laughing. Pieces of sandstone broke off in our hands, but we did get up a-ways.

I was the highest, standing up on a narrow ledge, with my left hand in a sizable crevice in the rock. Gave me a good enough grip to stay. I had writ "Jedediah" and had got up to carving the "R" in Barstow, when the ledge under my right foot gave way. Only smart thing I did was toss the knife off to the side. Jack Simpson broke my fall, but he himself landed hard on the base. My knees was a little bloody from scraping against the rock face, but nothing was broken or sprained bad. Charlie had been off to the side and seen it all happen. Scared him mightily, he said, seeing bodies flying down before his eyes. But it was Jack what was in trouble. Twisted his foot real bad.

We had passed a spring in a small grove of trees on our way to Chimney Rock. I found my knife, and then with me and Charlie supporting Jack, the three of us made our way real slow to that spring. It was clear and cold and a chance to get wet in a peaceable way. Weren't so peaceable, though, when we threw Jack in with all his clothes on. "Got to get that foot iced real fast!" we shouted. "We got a couple of miles back to camp." He took it in good spirits. Me and Charlie went in bare skin! It was shivery and tingle-y, and with all that splashing the three of us got to feeling real good.

We made it back to camp before supper. When we got Jack to the Simpson wagon, his mother made a poultice of wheat bran and vinegar, wrapped it in a cloth, and put it on his foot to bring down the swelling. "You are going to smell like souring pickles!" I shouted back at him when me and Charlie left. At my wagon, Mr. Henshaw hollered some, but I didn't pay too much mind. I'd got to go swimming for the first time on this trip by choice.

For anybody in the next generations reading this, that's how come our family name, or at least part of it, got to be up on Chimney Rock.

Later

Had a narrow escape tonight! I almost called Mr. Perkins "Mr. Grouch" to his face. I was sitting next to him at the campfire, when he asked me a question. I was so startled to hear him say something to me besides "Hmmph," I said. "Yessir, Mr. Gr . . ." and caught myself just in time. "Yessir, Mr. Perkins, I did truly go out to Chimney Rock. It was mighty awesome, sir."

"Tain't nothing but a haystack-shaped pile of rock with a pole jammed down the center of it!"

I shouldn't have expected anything else. Mama would have said, "That man is true to form." Mama would have also said Chimney Rock is truly one of the grand spectacles. When Pa would read the paper, she'd laugh at what she called the tall tales, but the sights like the Chimney she said was going to make the trip bearable. We'd be traveling so many days seeing the same grass in front of us, it would be a blessing to have the sights. Most times it was Pa who talked about adventuring, and Mama who worried about getting through each day. Every time Pa would speak of the "grandness of it all," Mama would say there's still the day-by-day. But she had been anticipating the sights. I wish she could've seen them.

*   *   *

I get through Mama's "day-by-day" real fast most of the time. There's the chores, of course, but if I get them done real quick, and get away before Mr. Henshaw comes up with something else for me, then there's time for adventuring.

I think I'm sounding like Pa.

June 17

We come on a camp of fur trappers today. They was layed by 'cause the river is so low, they can't float their boats down. They got sled heaps of buffalo and antelope and deer skins piled high as a grown man. Mr. Hall, the pilot-guide, told us at the noon stop that we'd be passing them up a-ways.

We stopped a real short time when we reached them. Captain Osborne and some of the councilmen talked with them. Our cattle, however, didn't want to mingle. They crossed the road away from the sleds. The oxen would have moved over, too, I think, if they weren't yoked up tight. I think they didn't like the smell of those animal skins. The ladies didn't much, either. Neither the skins nor the trappers. Missus Simpson come by. "Strangers to razors!" she said to Missus Henshaw. Then in a real loud voice she talked about Benjamin Franklin and cleanliness being next to Godliness.

I don't think the trappers paid her much mind. I wouldn't neither if I was them. Must be real special to be free like that. Don't have to answer to no one. Fix your traps as you needs, not when a Mr. Henshaw tells you to. You know when your horse is needing a rest, and you don't cripple it like a Mr. Henshaw. And you eat when you're hungry, roll up when you're tired. I could be a mountain man. They have real fine buckskin pants. Keeps off the thorns, Mr. Littleton says. I want to get me a pair.

Later

Mr. Fenster come by tonight to lend Missus Henshaw two books he was telling her about last Friday night at the dancing. One is about wild flower herbals and the other is about a kind of medicine called homeopathy. Mr. Henshaw was out with the hunting party, so things was pretty quiet. Missus Henshaw made a pot of tea, and we sat and listened to the story of the books.

They belonged to Rachel Fenster, Mr. Fenster's mother. Just before she died she gave them to him and said they had knowledge he was to treasure. He was not much older than me when she passed. He and his father left Germany and traveled to New York City. That's when I found out he sounded like someone who come from Germany.

Anyways, the whole time Mr. Fenster was on the ocean, he carried the books in a bag he slung over his shoulder. They was all he had left of his mother. Like me and Mama's journal, I guess. He's had them ever since.

"Sometimes I think passing on learning is the only real gift we can give our children," Missus Henshaw said. Mr. Fenster smiled and said he thought his mother would have liked Missus Henshaw.

Then he turned to me and said, "Jedediah, being accurate is part of learning. Many sayings come from your Mr. Franklin. 'Cleanliness is next to Godliness,' however, is not one of them." He went on to tell me it was pronounced in a famous sermon by the Methodist preacher John Wesley, who found it in the writings of the Hebrew fathers.

Missus Henshaw was listening all attentive, but I think Mr. Fenster talks too much, at least some of the time. I don't think I will tell Missus Simpson it weren't Benjamin Franklin.

June 18

I am on guard duty! Mr. Henshaw was supposed to be on duty tonight, but he sent me. Most of the men don't like standing guard 'cause it breaks their sleep. But they have to take turns doing it 'cause somebody's got to see the stock don't stray off or get stolen. Mr. Henshaw has done it, but tonight he was plumb angry at . . . I'm not even sure what. The grass was parched for much of the road, and we found no good water. Without feed and water for the animals, the Captain said we should keep pushing on. Mr. Henshaw couldn't make up his mind about anything. He wanted to push on, and he didn't. He said the Captain was right, and at the same time he was wrong. He was not just hollering at, but whupping Jake. Jake's our lead ox, and Missus Henshaw's particular partial to him. I think Mr. Henshaw was whupping at him just to spite her.

It was near midnight when we reached this spot. Mr. Henshaw grabs my sleeve and says, "I'm tired, boy, and you're gonna stay out there tonight!"

First time I ever seen Missus Henshaw steamy angry. "You are not going to send a boy to do a man's job," she said. "There's real dangers out there. You know the Bennetts and Morrisons both lost cows this past week. You know the Indians is thieving by night. Besides, there's wolves roaming in packs. You can't send the boy!"

"I'll do what I damn well please!" Then he stretched, yawned, and crawled inside the tent. Missus Henshaw looked at me and said real serious, "Keep your eyes open, Jedediah, and if you get sleepy, pinch your arm till it hurts."

I was happy she was looking out for me, but I was glad Mr. Henshaw didn't pay her no mind this time. I been wanting to stay up real late and see some wolves and maybe scare off some Indians.

So that's how I come to be sitting outside the corral now, waiting for something to happen. The wolves is howling real mournful-like. Not angry. Just mournful. Kind of gets right inside of you. Pa would have known how far away they are.

Later

I am too excited to sleep! I did have to pinch myself a couple of times like Missus Henshaw said, and it was a good thing. Mr. Henshaw told me where I was supposed to be. He said Mr. Welch and Ned Appleton was also guards, but that I wasn't supposed to be talking to them, just minding my own section. That's what I was doing. I'd been leaning up against a big rock, taking in the wolf howls and the wind in the grass and the few cleaning-up sounds from the corral behind me. Everything was sounding comfortable, when suddenly I got the strangest feeling back of my neck. Over to the left some fifteen or twenty yards away, there was a rustling that didn't sound quite right. Don't know exactly what was different — heavier, maybe. Anyways, I waited real still. The rustling would stop and then start up again.

Grass don't move like that by itself. So I got down real low and waited. When the rustling started again, it went on a bit longer before it stopped. It was getting real close to where I was crouched down. Then a dark shadow started to rise up. Before I realized what I was doing, I set up a hollering that would have raised the dead, as Mama used to say.

It raised the living this time, 'cause the shadow stood up sharp and started to run toward the bluff in the distance. Samuel Hall was by my side before I even finished hollering. He chased after the shadow, and was followed by three others from camp carrying torches. The Captain seemed surprised to see me, and asked where Mr. Henshaw was. When I told him, he pursed his lips like it didn't surprise him. Then he said some real nice things about my being alert and all that. He sent me back to camp and told me to get Mr. Henshaw and wait at his wagon. When I reached the tent, Mr. Henshaw was already up. I don't think anybody slept through all the commotion. He grumbled, but he come along to the Captain's wagon.

We weren't waiting but a few minutes when the men come back, pushing a man in front of them. "Hey, boy, looks like we got ourselves an Indian!" Mr. Henshaw said.

By then a group of others had gathered at the Captain's wagon. They brought the prisoner right up to the wagon. He was a strange-looking Indian. Bare-chested and wearing buckskin britches, but in the torchlight you could see his hair was light brown, and his face, arms, and legs was all greased up to look dark.

"What we got ourselves, Asa," Mr. Littleton said to Mr. Henshaw, "is a *white* Indian!"

By now some of the ladies had come up to the Captain's wagon. Everybody was murmuring about a white Indian. Jacob Fenster must have seen my confusion, 'cause he started explaining.

"You know, Jedediah, there's been times cows are missing and we don't know right off why. Some folks immediately say it's the Indians. Some of the time it is. Sometimes the animals wander off. You know that from yesterday morning's roundup. Mr. Bennett's heifer that fell down the ravine and got caught in the brush? And then there was Mr. Morrison's cow that went back to find its calf, the one he sold to the company we passed a-ways back?" I was remembering that one. "Mother-love," Missus Henshaw had said. Mr. Fenster went on, "It is true some of the times it is the Indians stealing . . ."

"But what's 'white Indians' got to do with it?" I interrupted.

"I'm getting there, Jedediah, I'm getting there. These are white men *pretending* to be Indians so that the Indians will be blamed."

"That's bad by two's, Mama would say!" I blurted out. "Thievin' *and* blamin' someone else for it." It was the first time I had said anything about my family out loud. It had slipped out.

Mr. Fenster was real quiet. "Your mama must have been a very smart woman," he said.

June 19

Slept much of today. The Captain gave Mr. Henshaw a talking-to about sending me out last night. He even said I might have done a better job than Mr. Henshaw, and so we was lucky in the end, but that if Mr. Henshaw missed guard duty again, he would be out of the company. Captain was still talking when I fell asleep.

June 20

The Taler twins were holding forth again tonight. We are camped near Scott's Bluffs by good water and grass and wood. So it's a good place. But the Talers say there's a "melancholy tradition" about the naming of the bluffs, and they kept us all round the campfire listening to the story and watching them tell it like a ball being tossed back and forth, back and forth. This is how I remember them telling it:

MICAH: Now some twenty years ago Hiram Scott was working for the Rocky Fur Company . . .

JEREMIAH: Actually, Micah, it was the American Fur Company, though there's some reports he was a hermit, never working a day for another soul.

MICAH: In any event, he was a young man . . .

JEREMIAH: Well now, brother, I heard he was an old mountaineer.

MICAH: In any event, he was traveling with companions and was killed by Indians . . .

JEREMIAH: Whatever you like, brother, and I 'pologize about correcting you, but the real truth is he died of starvation.

MICAH: In any event, he dragged himself over ground many miles until he reached . . .

JEREMIAH: Actually, it were his friends transported him, knowing as how he thought this a magnificent spot. . . . Sorry, Micah.

MICAH: In any event, his bones was found right here and . . .

JEREMIAH: . . . this place's been called Scott's Bluffs ever since. Right you are, brother!

Far as I can make out, some time in the past a man named Scott died somewheres around here.

June 22

We're at Fort Laramie! Captain Osborne says that means we're near 700 miles from Independence. It's the Sabbath, which means Preacher Turnbow is happy we are stopping over. But Mr. Simpson said he'd be surprised if too many would sit for too long at a service. It's late, and tomorrow morning we'll go up to the Fort real early.

June 23

There's so much to get done! Mr. Henshaw's looking to get our teams shoe-ed at the blacksmith here. He's aiming to get a cheap price, but Missus Henshaw has already walked about the Fort, and she says they are selling everything high. She was hoping to stock up on eggs, sugar, coffee, and tea, but it is too dear to buy very much. Mr. Henshaw snorted and said, they ain't met him yet. "Never seen a man I couldn't talk down!" I am sure that's 'cause he scarcely lets anybody complete a sentence. Only time I saw him quiet was when Captain Osborne talked to him the night I was a guard.

The Fort is several miles from the Platte and upstream from Laramie. We corralled about a mile away. There's level plains all around with a herd of buffalo grazing real peaceful off to the west. I was staring at the snowcapped mountain way off in the distance, when Mr. Henshaw grabbed me. "Quit dreamin', boy." He didn't need me, just didn't want me paying him no mind. I followed behind him into the Fort, which is a town built in a square with everything facing in on the square. In each doorway something else was going on. He went off to find the blacksmith. The ladies was shopping and trading at the dry goods. There was a number of storerooms, and in one shop the cobbler was working steady, resoling one pair of boots after another. Then, right in front of one stall was a pile of buffalo hides and buckskin clothes for sale. I truly need my boots fixed, but I headed for the skins. I been hungering after buckskin pants, but of course I had no money nor something to trade. So I was just looking.

A tall thin man with red hair sticking out all over his head and chin came from inside the stall and said it was four dollars for the pants. When I said I didn't have any money, he pointed at my knife and offered to trade. I was thinking, I can't trade my knife, I need it. Besides, Pa gave it to me and wouldn't be giving me anything else for the rest of my days. So I told him no.

Hiram Littleton was passing by at the time, and I guess he heard all this, 'cause he said something I couldn't believe. "Jedediah," he said, "I've been thinking, I could use an assistant, and I am looking to hire." Hire! He said, "We're headed into some rough country and there's going to be lots more things need fixing." I couldn't say, "Yessir!" fast enough, but then I remembered about Mr. Henshaw, and my heart sank, and I said I figured Mr. Henshaw'd got a lot for me to do.

That didn't stop Mr. Littleton. He said he'd work it out. Then as if having a job weren't enough, as he was about to leave, he handed me three dollars, saying it was an advance payment so we could shake hands on the arrangement! I stood there with the coins in my hand and stared after him. The tall man from the stall come out again. When he held his hand out, I gave him my three dollars, and that's how I got my buckskin pants and a job all at the same time!

Later

Seems the blacksmith told Mr. Henshaw to take his business elsewhere if he didn't like the prices. Of course there is no elsewhere. Missus Henshaw made him a cup of camomile tea to calm him down.

June 24

The trail has begun to change, just like Mr. Littleton said. We are moving into mountain country, though the only one we're seeing just yet is Laramie Peak in the distance. But it is truly a mountain. Sally would have said, "It's a confusion," seeing snow and ice on a burning hot day.

Lots of furniture and other belongings is being dropped by the side of the trail. I thought folks had lightened up as much as they could back at the Platte crossing. But seems there's always more to leave. Missus Henshaw left her mother's carved sewing chest, and has put all her needles and pins and threads in a basket. I think Mr. Henshaw's angry that I got nothing to discard. Bekky says I'm lucky 'cause I don't have no choices to make. She gave up one of her two dolls. I couldn't hardly believe what I saw then. When Bekky wasn't looking, Mr. Henshaw picked up one of those dolls she'd left and shoved it back in a chest!

Mid-day

Me and Charlie ate dinner over at the Sedlows. Afterward we come back with Lucy to pick up Bekky, and the four of us went off to pick berries. It's the only fresh fruit we've had since we finished off a few melons early on. Since then we've had only dried apples and peaches. We was eating so many berries, our fingers and mouths was all blue from the juice. And still we brought back a lot. Enough for Missus Sedlow and Missus Henshaw and Charlie's aunt to promise to make pies. Almost like a birthday celebration, Bekky said, and she was right.

June 27

I been going over to Mr. Littleton's wagon most days after dinner. Mr. Henshaw usually eats, smokes, and takes a nap at the nooning rest stop. Nobody complains, 'cause it's a nice quiet time.

We been following along the south side of the Platte, sometimes on the bottoms, and then up and down hillsides. It's a parched land these past days. Captain Osborne says we're at the end of the high plains and beginning the uphill journey to the Rocky Mountains. It's been hard finding grazing for the cattle. Passed a dead cow by the road. Buzzards and probably wolves have already started on it. Must have collapsed from exhaustion. It's not the first we've passed. Our teams are looking a bit thin and dusty, too. It'd be real hard if we lost any one of them, and a sadness, too. Spending all this time with them, they become part of your family.

Jack says his mother's been counting the people gravesites. Seen fourteen since we started out. But she's sure there's lots more, only they're covered up real good to keep them hidden from scavengers, man or beast. Mr. Littleton told me how they do it. Real careful, they cut out squares of turf. Then when they're digging the hole, they shovel all the dirt onto a blanket. They try to go down at least six feet, but that's hard 'cause there's so much rock. Anyways, they wrap the body in a blanket and lower it into the hole, putting all the dirt back on top of it. Then they replace the turf squares. Mr. Littleton says they try to do this near the trail so they can roll the wagon wheels over it. That way it looks like all the rest of the road. How many have died traveling west? I guess no one knows for sure. Nobody in our company besides Mama, Pa, and Sally.

I would have cut real fine squares for them. And dug deep no matter how long it took.

June 28

Charlie, Jack, and me was out adventuring, when we saw what looked like a platform raised on posts at least eight feet high. When we got closer, there was bodies lying up there in various states of decaying. It was an Indian cemetery up in the air! Nobody said a word. We turned around like we was one person and raced back to camp. We made it in a quarter the time it took us to get there. When we reached the wagons and stopped panting, Charlie said, "Maybe we should tell Missus Cavendish. In case she loses her coffin, there's another way." We laughed real hard and real nervous.

Later

At the campfire tonight Jack and me and Charlie was talking about what a sight that was we saw. "If you're in the ground," Charlie said, "your ghost ain't out loose wandering around."

"Do you think we was bumping into any Indian ghosts?" Jack asked.

That was not a thought I appreciated. But then I remembered something. "I always heard ghosts make themselves known to you when they're there. That's their whole reason for being, ain't it?"

We concluded maybe coffins was a good idea. Then Jack said his father told him the Indians put up scaffolds like we saw so their bodies don't get dug up and mutilated by the animals. That sounded pretty good, too, seeing as how we're breaking shovels to get down real deep to avoid the same thing.

June 29

Mr. Littleton's showing me how to fix my boots. Didn't seem to me that was really helping him with *his* work, but he said it was. He needs an assistant he says who feels good so he can focus on other people's broken things. Leastwise that's how I understood what he was saying. He showed me how to cut out a leather sole from a hide to fit over my boot bottoms. I used a small awl to make holes all around the edges. With a strip of sinew I stitched the sole onto the boot. I still go barefoot when it's real sandy, but now I'm prepared for the rough sage. We have already walked through some, and Mr. Littleton says there's a lot more to come.

Mr. Littleton has a full set of tools for carving wood,

leather, and even working metal. I think I'd like to be a master craftsman like he was back in the States.

July 1

Another ox down. A crew of men is out searching for three cows gone missing. Two that was rounded up don't belong to us. Captain says we're likely to find a trail message if another company is missing cattle. He says we should know in a day or so.

There's been a lot of game along the river. The hunting party come back with two elk and three deer. I still haven't gone out with them. Mr. Henshaw usually goes, and so it's always a good time for me to work with Mr. Littleton. We've been repairing wagon wheels quite regular this past week. Even Amos has been helping a little, keeping all the tools in their right places. It's been so dry, the wheels shrink and don't fit the iron. Mr. Littleton has the men soaking the wheels overnight, which gives them back a little life. And we've been cutting down the rings, and wedging. Captain was telling Mr. Hall when I come by with a message how lucky this company is to have someone like Mr. Littleton. Made me feel real good to be working with him.

July 2

The dust has been getting to everybody. I been wiping the noses of our team 'cause they're having trouble breathing like the rest of us. I saw Mr. Fenster do that, but Mr. Henshaw didn't want me to. This morning he grabbed the rag out of my hand and snarled that if I paid as much attention to his needs as to these dumb animals, I'd make it a lot easier for myself.

They may be dumb, but they're a lot nicer to do something for than Mr. Henshaw. They don't ask and they don't holler. They keep on working every day, steaming hot or cold, rain or hail, fog or sun, sand, and now this prickly sage. I don't have their patience. He's been hollering at Missus Henshaw. Bekky gets quiet and clings to her mama's apron. Mr. Henshaw doesn't hit Bekky, but he frightens her real bad, though he doesn't seem to notice. I never think fast enough to say something when it's happening. And later is too late, as Mama used to say.

Mid-day

We nooned in a sandstorm. The dust was swirling about while we took things off the wagon for Missus Henshaw to get dinner. Mr. Henshaw went off to smoke by the river. If he was captured and tortured by the Indians, I wouldn't be sorry. But all the Indians we met so far don't seem like the torturing kind. More talking and trading. I wonder if wishing for something bad that you know won't happen makes the wishing of a bad thing not so bad?

Later

The sand got to Missus Henshaw. I think it's all his hollering, too. Anyways, when there was more sand at suppertime, she threw down the kettle, pulled off her apron, and started to cry. Then she looked up and said in a fierce voice to no one in particular, "Leave me alone!" and ran off into the flats.

Mr. Henshaw looked after her, but did nothing 'cept tell me to get supper ready. I put some jerky out with dried fruit, set the coffeepot going, picked up Bekky, and went over to the Sedlows. I figured since Lucy's sisters was around Bekky's age, maybe Missus Sedlow wouldn't mind one more. She was real kind about it and put Bekky down next to her two little ones. She said Bekky would stay the night, and I should tell Missus Henshaw when I saw her not to worry.

Two or three hours must have passed before Missus Henshaw come back. She was calm and real quiet. She walked past Mr. Henshaw, who was staring at her, and went right over to the fire. She got the coffeepot going again and turned to me. "I'm sorry, Jedediah. I don't like to lose my temper." She turned to Mr. Henshaw. "I apologize to both of you." Mr. Henshaw chewed down real hard on a piece of tobacco, but said nothing. It is a rarity he's speechless.

Pa always said it takes a strong person to say they been wrong.

July 3

When Mr. Hall was scouting ahead early today, he saw a marker. It was a piece of yellow cloth with writing on it, and it was wedged between two rocks at the side of the road. Captain Osborne showed it at the council meeting this morning. Seems the company up ahead is missing several cows. So I guess the extra ones the men rounded up belong to them. Someone from that company will come back in a day or two to see if anybody's found them.

Missus Simpson and some of the other ladies was at the meeting. This was most unusual, since ladies don't go to the council. But they said they knew we was close to Independence Rock and wanted to know if we'd be there for our national day of independence. Captain said he weren't certain, but if so, it would be late at night before we arrived. The ladies is surely planning something.

July 4

The men did a thirteen-gun salute at sunrise, but that is all for today. We're not celebrating till we get to Independence Rock. Captain says we'll be there tomorrow, and then we will lay by. Me and Charlie and Jack is ready for a big party.

July 5

It's a big round turtle with its head tucked in its shell, sitting in the middle of the plains, this Independence Rock. And we are finally here! Missus Henshaw's been washing up since we corralled. It's mid-day, and dinner, the ladies say, is the beginning of the big party. They have been working for days, and we got any kind of pie you can think of! Mince-meat, goose-berry, choke-berry, currant pie. We got lemon cake, spice cake, apple cake. There is pickles and fresh antelope meat and mashed potatoes, and bottles of flavored brandies for the ladies, whisky for the men, and honeyed milk for us. Everything is layed out on barrels and tubs upturned, and you just wander from place to place, taking tastes at each stop. Even the jerked strips is arranged to look inviting on platters that was unpacked special for today.

The Taler twins is harmonizing, and people are bringing platters to them so they'll keep on without stopping except for a bite now and then. Charlie and Jack and the other boys is getting ready for a ball game, but I got something else to do first. I told Missus Henshaw I'd take Bekky for a tour around the platters. Lucy had her little sisters with her, so we could keep an eye on the three of them. This way Missus Henshaw and Missus Sedlow could keep laying things out. And the more they lay out, the more there is to eat!

Bekky said she planned to taste all the berry pies first 'cause it was safer than trying to save room for the sweets at the end. She's a smart one. "Mama said I could have dessert first today, seeing as how it's a ce-re-bratious occasion!" She was smiling, real happy.

"Ain't it the truth! This here's some C-E-R-E-BR-A-SH-U-N!" The words were sloshing out of Mr. Henshaw. He had started his celebrating early. Missus Henshaw put her arm around his waist and tried to steer him to the wagon. "I'm party-ing, woman!" he shouted as he pulled away from her, waving a whisky bottle. Jacob Fenster was watching. I gave Bekky to Lucy and got Mr. Henshaw by the elbow.

"Hey, boy! How's about a drink!" He was leaning heavy on me. We moved toward the wagon. He wasn't yelling now, just mumbling over and over, "I'm tired. Dog tired." He leaned up against the wagon and slid down to the ground. I moved some baskets and chests around so I could lay out a blanket roll on the wagon bed. Mr. Fenster had come up. It took a while for us to get Mr. Henshaw inside the wagon, but he was snoring before his head touched the blanket. Laying like that, breathing deep, he looked like he'd shrunk in size half a foot. I remember Pa saying, "A drunk's a pitiful sight."

Later

I am so full, I feel like a puffed-up grouse. I guess Mr. Henshaw's still sleeping, 'cause he never showed up again. Missus Simpson and Missus Henshaw's finally sitting down. Mr. Fenster's been over by them every time I passed by. The Reverend has been speechifying, and even the Captain said a few words about "our nation's Jubilee of Liberty!" There was speeches with every toast. More speeches than a body wants to remember, and lots of cheering, which we boys did.

It seems most everybody was having a good time today. Excepting, of course, Mr. Grouch. He stopped me and Charlie as we was running past. "You boys heard about that young fella Lovejoy?" That was hard to pass by. Me and Charlie plunked ourselves down. Weren't going to miss ole Mr. Grouch speechifying!

"Well, seems like Lovejoy," he said, "was fool enough to climb up that there pile of Independence Rock. And fool enough like all you young fellas to think he could carve his name into posterity." His eyes glinted. "Well, young sirs, he got his posterity all right!" he cackled happily. "He had just finished carving 'LOVE' and was beginning on the 'JOY,' when a band of Indians swept past, pulled him off of his posterity, tied him up, and dragged him *humiliated* to his camp. Then they sold him back to his own company for three *cows*!" Mr. Grouch made sure we didn't miss "humiliated" and "cows."

And if that weren't enough, he added to no one in particular, "I'll be glad to join a 'Jubilee of Liberty,' when I am liberated from wagons and wheels and dust and bacon and beans and mus-KEE-tows!"

Everybody had something to say. That's the kind of day it was.

July 6

At the council meeting this morning, the Captain reported, "As you all know, we have left the mighty, muddy Platte, and we are now by the Sweet Water River." I guess that's important information for the Captain for leading and Mr. Hall for scouting, but the only difference I can see is the Sweet Water is clear and the Platte was muddy. Mr. Fenster, though, made me catch my breath when he said, "That means, doesn't it, Captain, that we are almost halfway on our journey?" I stared at Mr. Fenster and then I waited for the answer. When Captain Osborne nodded, I didn't hear another thing anybody said.

I am nearly halfway through Mama and Pa's Grand Adventure, and they don't know it. I headed back to the wagon.

Mr. Henshaw missed the meeting, and seeing as how I been there, at least part of the time, he wanted a report. He's back to his regular size, but I guess his head aches too much for him to be back to regular hollering just yet. Missus Henshaw has a smile like she's thinking about something real nice that's not here and now.

Later

We was passing Devil's Gate, Mr. Sedlow said. Devil's Gate! What is Bekky going to make of that? Me and Charlie and Jack decided we was going over to see this Devil's Gate. Lucy wanted to come. We had all finished morning chores, and figured nobody would miss us for the short side trip. We'd catch up to the wagons well before nooning.

The Devil's Gate is where the Sweet Water has carved right through a spur in the mountain. Mr. Littleton says the mountain must be four or 500 feet high. Don't think I can explain to Bekky how water can be so strong, it cuts through solid rock. Don't really understand it myself. We scrambled up the granite cliff and peered down. Then I got a better understanding. From up on top you could see the river pouring in the canyon mouth with such force, it looked like it could *move* a mountain, not just split it. Charlie said he was dizzy, and sat with his back to the gap.

The river flows calm before it enters the channel, and then it turns into a monstrous side-ways, upside-down thunderstorm, where the rains pour horizontal, and the spray shoots up the sides. Jack and me said Charlie was a fraidy-cat, but I was feeling a little light-headed myself.

When I looked at Lucy and Jack, I know we was all glad to be going down and getting back to the wagons.

I think only Bekky missed us. "Jed! Jed! I want a drink of the real Sweet Water!"

"Me, too, Bekky," I said. Maybe this time something would be like its name. "We'll try it when we noon," I promised.

It was not sweet. Just ordinary water, and Bekky was mighty disappointed. So I told her about the Devil's Gate, and how the Evil One was spitting so fierce in that canyon you could feel his breath on your face. "Made you wet," I said. "See, I come back all sweaty?" She nodded, her eyes big and round.

Evening-time

I was glad Bekky was asleep when the Taler twins told *their* story about Devil's Gate. We was all sitting round the central campfire when Jeremiah began:

"There's an ancient Indian legend," he whispered, almost like a hiss, "that has been passed from father to son, mother to daughter, down through the mists of time. The story they tell is this: Once, long, long ago when the land was still filled with monsters, a powerful and fearsome behemoth roamed this valley. It had seventy-five-foot-long tusks that curved and twisted over and around, ending in deadly sharp spears."

Jeremiah paused and stared into the fire. We waited.

"Just by a flick of its tail," Micah continued, "the river would flood its banks. The storm of its breath would drive the other animals from the land. This mammoth beast terrified and tormented all the peoples. They could neither dwell in peace nor hunt in need. A wise man of the tribes warned them to destroy it. 'The Great Spirit wills it so. Ignore this command and you will be annihilated!' he prophesied."

Charlie whispered, "What's 'annihilated'?"
"Don't know. But something fearsome!"

"And so they plotted and planned," continued Jeremiah. "The attack would take place at dawn. Warriors climbed the mountains, descended to the bottom of the valleys, hid in the rocky outcrops. As the first hint of red marked the horizon on the designated morning, the behemoth rose from its bed in the river. A rain of arrows poured down on it from every direction! It flayed and bellowed. It twisted and turned, but the onslaught went on and on and on. Blinded with rage, the beast reared up. With a mighty roar it charged toward the mountain, lowered its head, and thrust forth its deadly tusks. The mountain was torn apart and the behemoth vanished into the gap!"

Then the twins said in unison, "Never to be seen again!"

We sat stunned. The silence was broken only by the cracking of the embers in the dying fire. Later, rolled up tight in my blanket under the wagon, I tried to keep my eyes open as long as I could. I was afraid of dreaming.

July 7: Early morning

I dreamt I was standing on top of a mountain with each foot on a snow-covered peak. Clouds was moving in fast like someone was pulling a shade across the sky. In front of my mountain way far in the distance, a darkness was rolling toward me. As it got closer, I could see it was a head of surging water, carrying along all manner of things. A wheel spun on the waves, and tree trunks vaulted forward and back. Empty drawers slid in and out of a chest. Foam steamed up and heated the air about my head. Water streamed from my eyes and ears, and when I opened my mouth to cry out, a rainbow curved out like a ram's horn.

The mountain began to shake and shudder. I felt the

wrench of the cracking rocks shoot up my back even before I heard it. I was tossed down on the foam, and each shaft of spray was a knife prick on my skin. Suddenly, there was total stillness, and a piercing light. I was leading a flock of birds by a vast ocean.

July 9

For the past two days we have crisscrossed back and forth over the Sweet Water. We can see snowy mountains in the distance, but the road has been dry and dusty, which is mighty irritating. Mr. Henshaw is back to hollering at full strength. This morning at breakfast, he kept banging his tin cup on a rock, muttering, "Damn dust! God forsaken land! Damn dust!"

"Asa," Missus Henshaw said, exasperated. "I think that's enough cussing in front of the children."

He looked at me and snorted. Then he banged and cussed again, and a chip of the rock flew off. Bekky ran under the wagon and pulled her apron over her head. I jumped up. "You're frightening her!" I shouted. "You gotta stop!" I couldn't believe I said something. I don't know what startled him more, me saying anything at all, or saying something particular about Bekky.

He glanced quickly at her crouching under the wagon,

grunted, and went off. Missus Henshaw said quietly, "He don't mean no real harm." But she looked tired.

Mid-day

Mr. Littleton's showing me how to cut a dovetail joint. "Makes a real tight fitting," he says. I'm fixin' Missus Henshaw's grub box.

I was asking Mr. Littleton if he remembers his dreaming. He said he's too tired at night to be spending time on pictures. He needs his sleep. If he'd had my dream, he'd be needing even more sleep! But I'm not planning on telling it.

Later

When I took Bekky to the Sedlows' wagon to play with Lucy's sisters, she said to me in a real little voice, "Papa didn't always used to holler." Like she wanted me to understand something. "He made me toys and I'd sit on his knee when Mama'd sing at night." The Sedlow girls shouted at Bekky to hurry up, and she ran off.

July 11

We keep walking through dry sage and sandy plains. And I kept taking my boots off and putting them back on. We reached a marshy bottom, and the Captain decided to stop. The sun had baked us dry by the time we got there. Mr. Fenster took one of them river poles of his and pushed down into the marshy grass. He hit a bed of solid ice! Captain said he had heard about these ice springs. The men gave us boys the shovels, and we dug down about a foot and a half to the ice layer. We filled up pails with chunks, which we put in the water barrels, making "DEE-cious ice-water!" Bekky said. She's right. It's just perfect on a steaming hot day.

July 12

We have left the Sweet Water and are on the climb to the Rocky Mountains. Bekky says she can't feel us going up, and she's right. It's so gradual, you hardly know you are climbing.

Mid-day

We nooned just over South Pass, which Mr. Littleton says is the dividing ridge separating the waters flowing into the Atlantic and those flowing to the Pacific. It was disappointing 'cause it don't stand out. You can see so far to each side, it don't feel like you're going through something at all.

Captain says we'll be coming on Pacific Springs soon, which is the first westward-running water. Now *that'll* be something to see.

Corral

We started down a real easy descent and arrived at the springs, which Lucy says are flowing like us toward the great Pacific Ocean! The grazing here is good, and we're setting up camp.

After we unyoked and started unpacking the wagons, Captain Osborne held up a bottle of whisky. He turned westward, raised the bottle up. "Hail to Oregon!" Then he passed the bottle around to all the men. There were lots of "Hip Hip Hoorays!" Excepting Mr. Grouch, who grumbled the Captain should save the whisky till we get there. Nobody paid him much mind, except ole Missus Cavendish. She stuck her finger in his bony chest: "If you don't start enjoying something, Jasper Perkins, you are going to be shriveled and dried up like a long-gone prune!"

Even Missus Henshaw looked happy. She said, "It's hard to remember some days where you're going, and why. But at a time like this, you remember real clear." Mr. Henshaw had a strange look on his face. It might have been a smile.

So we are in the Oregon country now. I don't have whisky and don't feel like cheering. I feel like crying, which I won't do. I won't. I miss you, Mama and Pa. You, too, Sally.

July 14

It's been real cold at nights. Got up this morning and there was ice one-fourth of an inch thick in the water bucket. Mr. Henshaw scooped up some of last night's beans and went off with the men to hunt antelope. We're out of buffalo range. I didn't get to hunt buffalo, but at least I got to see 'em and taste 'em.

Mr. Littleton's happy there'll be no more buffalo killing. He hasn't said anything yet about antelope.

Later

Several oxen is down. This time it's the alkali that's poisoning them. They drink the water that's got alkali and graze on the grasses that got deposits of the miserable white stuff from the overflowing water. It's a real sadness to see their stomachs all swelled out and a-bulging between their forelegs. Captain says it's the cough, though, that will kill them. He says the alkali water may get real bad from now on.

Mr. Fenster's got a cure if you catch the alkali early. He gets the cattle on their backs, which is not hard, since they are feeling so miserable and they don't put up much of a struggle. Then he pours grease down their throats. Seems to give them immediate relief, but like he says, only if the disease is just starting.

The Simpsons lost three cows, the Pringles, two, Charlie's uncle Mr. Welch, four, and us, one.

Missus Henshaw's eyes was tearing up when we drove past our cow. She told me to keep special watch on Jake to see what he's eating.

July 15

Haven't seen much of Ned Appleton lately. He's been spending a lot of time I guess with that Abigail Pringle.

Layed over looking for stray cattle. Puts the men in a foul mind. The ladies took the chance to wash up, and me and some of the boys helped them get the kettles going. Then we took off on the search. Didn't finish the roundup till near half past nine tonight. Captain says we'll be starting real early tomorrow.

July 17

When we stopped mid-day, there was real disagreement at a special council meeting Captain called. Seems we've been following the Little Sandy Creek headed toward the Big Sandy, and then on to the Green River. Mr. Simpson scratched out the trail in the ground. Then he showed a way to cut straight across to hit the Green. Would save nearly three days, he said. Looks like one of those triangle drawings coming up in my sums book. Pa was talking to me about this geometry being a way to solve some traveling questions, but he never got to explaining it.

Anyways, some of the men argued that we'd save days

if we cut straight across, but Captain said there wasn't water for forty miles if we took the shortcut. They went round and round arguing like that until finally they decided to stick with the Captain. So we been heading the longer, surer route.

I'm glad we're following the river 'cause we been catching lots of fish, and Missus Henshaw's been cooking them up real nice. Don't mind if I never see a piece of bacon again.

July 19

We been traveling along the Green. It's a clear stream, but the current's pretty fast and it looks to be a long way to the west bank. Nooned at a grassy-bottom site, where Captain Osborne said we'd cross. He got the men together to figure out the fording. He had Mr. Fenster draw a picture of it on the ground.

He made all these different triangles in the dust and explained how you could figure out how wide the stream was just by doing some numbers figuring. Then you'd know how much rope the lead horses would take across to set up a pull line. Takes real smart men like Mr. Fenster and the Captain to work this out. I studied Mr. Fenster's triangles real hard. It looked complicated, but when he explained it, it was real clear. If this is what Pa said was geometry, it is truly something to ponder! Captain says surveyors do this all the time. I think I would like to be a surveyor.

After Mr. Fenster did the drawing and explanation, we spent the rest of the day getting the wagon beds ready to float over. Mr. Henshaw was muttering about all the time wasted by having Jacob Fenster make the diagram. Nothing but "showin' off!" he called it.

Missus Henshaw said it was worth the time to be safe. She started talking 'bout the company we passed that was burying a little girl who died of a snakebite. Mr. Henshaw snapped at her that snakes got nothing to do with this here crossing.

But she kept right on, saying safety of the children is what's important, and that's what she was talking about. Bekky didn't hear none of this 'cause she was with Lucy and six other little ones learning their A-B-Cs.

Much later

All through the crossing I was studying a picture of Mr. Fenster's drawing in my mind. I guess I was so busy I didn't think about the Kaw until now.

July 21

Mr. Henshaw's getting meaner, if you can imagine it. Pinched me real hard this morning on the way to roundup. Said I was getting on his nerves, and he had a good mind to whup me. That was something Pa did once and never again. He said it de-based him, him being a grown man to beat up on a boy. I asked Mama what de-based was. From what she said I guess Pa meant you lower yourself by picking on someone smaller and weaker. I don't think Mr. Henshaw knows he is de-based.

July 22

We left the Green and are cutting across to Bridger's Fort. Captain said this morning we'd be there by tomorrow. I know Missus Henshaw is looking forward to stopping. We're out of sugar, and that makes Mr. Henshaw mad. It's his own fault for taking big scoops, but you can't tell him that.

Mid-day

Lucy has been teaching a class of little ones, including Bekky. Sometimes it's just before their bedtime and sometimes when we're nooning. We can see her from Mr. Littleton's wagon when I'm over there working. I didn't tell Mr. Littleton that Lucy's been correcting my grammar. It's the plurals and singulars she says I have trouble with. Seems whatever it should be, I'm partial to the other.

Mr. Littleton says he's impressed with her. Says she is a smart one and will make someone a real good wife. Can't imagine she's thinking about marrying. Who wants to get married?

Later

Ned Appleton wants to get married. Him and Abigail Pringle. They said something at the campfire tonight. What's he doing that for? It's all anybody's talking about. Me and Charlie's real tired of it. Ole Missus Cavendish says she's putting together a true-so. That's French, she says, for wedding clothes for Abigail. They're going to have the wedding at Fort Bridger, where there'll be a big party. Mr. Simpson said it was about time, they been mooning so long. Mr. Littleton is making a chest for them. All the ladies is excited about filling up the chest with stuff for the "newly-weds." Missus Henshaw was sure it was a good omen they were starting out fresh in a new country. Mr. Henshaw said he couldn't care less. First time I think he's right, but I won't say anything.

Mr. Grouch hmmph-ed several times. Said Ned was only doing it for the land. I asked Mr. Fenster about that. He said a man can get more than 300 acres just by going out to Oregon and settling. And he can double that if he's got a wife! "Well, that's the best reason I heard to do it," I said.

Mr. Fenster scratched his beard. "I'm not sure I'd want to be sitting through long winter nights in a house with someone who was only there because she got me some extra land." I hadn't thought about that.

July 23

We're here at the Fort, and the ladies have been bustling since we arrived. We're camped outside and will stay here through the wedding and party tonight. Haven't been to the Fort yet. Looks the same as Fort Laramie, but more run down. Dried clay over poles, and twenty-some cabins for the traders and their Indian wives. Captain says they got robes, dressed skins, pants, moccasins, and other fixin's, which the women here make real fine. But there's no time for looking yet 'cause the ladies sent me, Charlie, Jack, and some of the other boys out to catch trout for the wedding supper.

Later

The wedding's over. The best part was the trout we brought back. The ladies cooked them up special with mashed-up potatoes and stewed fruits. There was cakes and pies till you'd bust.

Mr. Henshaw and Mr. Grouch were talking together part of the time. Probably outdoing each other on what a bad idea getting married is. Ned's been smiling all afternoon, and Abigail ~~Pringle~~ Appleton did look real pretty in the dress they fixed up for her.

July 24

There's a lot of wagons people in other companies abandoned or sold to the traders at the Fort. Ned found one he thinks he can fix up pretty quick for him and Abigail. Mr. Littleton has me looking for parts for fixing our company's wagons. But since we can only do so much, the Fort's blacksmith and carpenter is getting a fair amount of work from our people.

Captain says we're heading out this afternoon.

July 25

I think I know why Jasper Perkins is a grouch! Yesterday, before the wedding ceremony, he come to Mr. Littleton's wagon, looking real peculiar with his bottom lip all squooshed in. Like he'd drunk a barrel of sour milk. He had something wrapped in a cloth that he handed to Mr. Littleton. "Hiram, can you please help me? They's been making me bleed." I was staring at the cloth wondering what could it be that's making Mr. Grouch ask somebody for something. And saying, "Please"!

When Mr. Littleton opened the cloth, my eyeballs about shot out of my head. Sitting in his hand was Mr. Grouch's bottom teeth, set up like a row of yellowing stones on a wooden bed!

"The frame sides are wearing down, making the fit unsteady," Mr. Littleton explained as he turned Mr. Grouch's teeth every which way. "You know, Jasper, they can make them out of porcelain now," he said. "When we get to Oregon City, I'm sure they'll mail you a set from

Philadelphia where I read they are doing all this new work on teeth. Wouldn't be exactly your measurements, but has to be better than this." He pointed to the right side of the frame. "Looks like there's been some splintering here."

"Yessiree, that's where the most bleedin's coming from. Be beholden if you could do something." I stared after him as he walked away. He looked like an old man.

July 28

For days we've been walking through dried-up stony country. Been up and down hills and crossing prickly sage. It's very bad grazing for the animals. For the past two nights we had to push through until late, just to find food for the poor creatures. Jake is not doing well, and Missus Henshaw's real worried we might lose him. You can see him limping. Mr. Henshaw stomps along the side, not saying much. Which I am not complaining about.

Later

Bekky cried when we took the yoke off Jake. We needed a couple of the men to move him over to the side of the road. Missus Henshaw was holding Bekky. "He gave us his all," she said. "No creature can do more in this life." Mr. Henshaw is back looking over the stock to bring up the strongest cow we can put under yoke.

July 29

This was a day you could use a smart ox like Jake. We come up a steep ridge, then down a sloping ravine. But it was the second mountain that caused all the problems. We was yoking and unyoking all afternoon. Each wagon was double-teamed to get a real good pull up. That's how steep it was. When we finally was all at the top, we went along the ridge for a couple of miles and then started down.

This is the steepest slope we been on. Had to brake the wheels with poles. We unyoked so the teams could be taken down without getting pushed by the wagons. Then with a couple of the men holding a rope twisted round a tree on top, they lowered each wagon down.

It's a miracle only one got broken up bad. The Welches'. Charlie said his uncle is cutting the wagon bed in half, leaving one set of wheels. They've left a lot of stuff scattered on the mountainside. There won't be room for much in the cart they're fashioning. Mr. Littleton and me has been working on framing a new bed for the cart. Charlie's worried about his aunt who's been riding in the wagon these last days 'cause she's been feeling poorly. Maybe Mr. Fenster has some special tea she can drink to build up her strength.

July 31

All the ladies is riding in the wagons, 'cause we been walking on crickets, millions of them for a couple of miles. They are covering everything. Most are about two inches long with huge legs. It's the legs Bekky can't stand to look at. These leaping critters are blanketing the ground as far as your eye can see. They are even hanging on the stalks of the sage.

We are crunching with every step. Saw Lucy walking. She does not look happy. I don't mind it, though I am getting tired of the noise.

August 1

At the council meeting this morning, Captain said we'd reach Soda Springs just before mid-day. First sight we got were several huge mounds of hard soda stone, with springs oozing out the top. Mr. Fenster said every time the water bubbles up, it leaves a little deposit, which turns into a real hard crust, which just keeps building up. Bekky asked if they'd grow so high, the tops would get stuck in the clouds. I told her that if that happened, the spring water would probably come down as rain. But right now the mounds are only as high as about seven Bekkys end to end. That's how I used to tell Sally how far away or tall something was. Been thinking a lot about Sally these last days. She would have tried to rescue some of the crickets, and she would have loved these oozing towers. They would've been one of Mama's sights, too.

Mid-day

Me and Charlie ~~is~~ are real excited we're nooning here. It's hard to remember this plural business. Anyways, the men have been talking about this special water for days now. The ladies are taking advantage of the springs for a small washing up, so we had a cold lunch. Mr. Littleton said I didn't have to work this noon, so we're off! Lucy's coming with us.

Later

The water just bubbles up all along the stream, sometimes rising up half a foot. With a little sugar added, it tastes as good as any soda water. Charlie and me were having a burping contest. Lucy was burping, too, but she says we're much worse 'cause we were doing it on purpose. She can't help herself. Neither can we, but we didn't tell her that.

Near the bank of the Bear River there's another spring that heaves up water and steam every few minutes. It comes out of a two-foot-high cone that's about three feet wide at the base. Lucy says it sounds like the steamboats whistling and puffing down the Mississippi River. Right near the puffer there's a hole in the ground. Whenever the steamboat whistles, gusts of steam and spray shoot out of this hole. I put my hat over it to see if more would come out of the puffer by corking this one up.

The top of my hat started inching up, but I was holding it down tight. BOOM! The steam shot a hole straight through and hurled me back a few feet. When Lucy and Charlie stopped laughing, Lucy said she'd see if she could weave me a new hat from grasses she gathered along the Platte.

Suppertime

Some of the men got a little cheerful tonight. They was mixing the soda water with some whisky, and having a fine old time. Mr. Littleton says every now and then a body needs to let off steam. Just like those springs, I guess.

August 4

Mr. Henshaw had a bad head again this morning. The only thing good about it is he aches too bad to yell. Except for the moaning escaping his lips, all is peace and quiet at the wagon. He missed the council meeting this morning, so I gave him a report. We'll be nooning at Fort Hall.

Mid-day

Captain Grant is in charge of the Fort for the Hudson's Bay Company, and he was very welcoming to us. Inside the Fort the Indian women had piles of clothes made from deer and antelope skins. They had woven into them different colored beads and porcupine quills. They were real nice-looking. I been saving up my pay from Mr. Littleton, and after I worked off the three dollars he gave me at Fort Laramie, I have nearly two dollars. Thought I might get me a real hat.

Then I saw these beautiful moccasins with blue and yellow and red beads. They looked like they'd fit Bekky, and I know she would love them with all the pretty beads. I guess I'll wait for Lucy's hat.

Later

The ladies have been buying and trading for flour, which we are real low on, but the men are doing hardly anything but talk in this place. On one side of the inner courtyard, a Mr. Randall was holding forth about the wonders of Oregon. I'd heard that kind of talk with Pa back home, so I went across the square to listen to another speaker. This was a Mr. Latherbee who said he'd been an army scout and that nothing was as wonderful as California. He started warning that most of us would never make it to Oregon. He said crossing the Snake River was perilous beyond anything we had experienced up to now. And if the river didn't get us, the Indians would. I thought there was going to be a shouting match across the courtyard.

We're losing seven families 'cause of Mr. Latherbee's

speechifying. Mr. Littleton said he was sure the California talker was in the pay of the Hudson's Bay Company. He says the British are trying to keep Americans out of the Oregon Territory. I don't know, Mr. Latherbee sounded pretty convincing. Might have persuaded Mr. Henshaw if he had heard him. But he was off someplace. He's been away a lot from the wagon, and Missus Henshaw and me have been spelling each other walking the team. She's looking real tired these days. If I'd have had more money, I would have got her a pair of moccasins, too.

Suppertime

Bekky loves the moccasins. Sally would have, too.

August 7

We've been traveling through what Mr. Fenster calls the great Snake River desert. The river itself is clear and runs strong over a pebbly bottom, and we fished a lot in it when we was at the Fort. But now we don't get down to it too much. It's deep in a ravine, cutting through rocks.

The last few days Mr. Fenster has come by at the midday stop to help with the oxen. He says this place puts him in mind of a poem called "The Rime of the Ancient Mariner," by a man named Samuel Coleridge. "Water, water, everywhere, nor any drop to drink." Puts me in mind of that, too, now that I hear it.

August 8

Mr. Henshaw slept in the wagon after we got yoked up this morning. This is the second time. Bad head again. He's still in there. Bekky's with Lucy, so it's just me and the missus. She was telling me how they come to be going to Oregon. Missus Henshaw's brother went out two years ago with that big company led by Dr. Marcus Whitman. He's preaching out there to the Indians, but he come back to preach to Americans about the wonders of Oregon. Anyways, Missus Henshaw got a letter from her brother this past fall right when the crop failed and right when it looked like they was going to lose everything. But before the bank got on them, Mr. Henshaw sold the farm. They didn't get all it was worth, but enough to pay off the loans and outfit for the trip. So she's hoping for a new life.

Don't seem to me like Mr. Henshaw's hoping for much of anything.

Mid-day

When I was working with Mr. Littleton, we could hear
Mr. Fenster reading out loud over at the Sedlows. The lit-
tle ones was listening real careful to the story of that an-
cient sailor. Amos Littleton was over there with them.
Even Missus Henshaw brought Bekky to hear the story.
"He's a fine reader," Mr. Littleton said. He looked sad.

August 9

The wagons going to California left us today. The seven
from our train joined up with a California company they
met at Fort Hall. I think there was twenty-seven of them
altogether. That leaves us with twenty-eight, actually
twenty-seven and a half, counting the Welches' cart as
half. I wonder what their trip will be like. Mr. Latherbee
only talked about our hard crossings of rivers and mountains, but Captain says there's some mighty rough country going to California. Mountains and deserts that may
be worse than what we'll be going through. Right now
it's hard to say, 'cause we been walking through stones
and dust for a long time. Mr. Simpson says this trail could
put a soul in mind of California. The minute he said it, I

knew if I'd be the last one in the company, I'd walk to Oregon alone. Don't know why. It just come to me.

August 10

Mr. Henshaw's up today. Mr. Fenster's fixed a special herb drink for him last night, and today his eyes aren't so clouded over. He was actually apologizing to Missus Henshaw this morning. Sort of. She was smiling when she poured out the coffee. When he saw me standing there, he hollered for me to get busy and adjust the harness. Guess he don't want me to hear him talking even a little nice.

Lucy's made me a hat. Fits comfortable. And today I found out why Missus Welch has been so poorly. Lucy told me. She said she's carrying, and her time's in less than a month. When I said that was going to be something fine, she looked at me like I was real dumb. "You haven't ever been stuck in a wagon with a crying baby, have you now, Jed Barstow?"

Mid-day

Amos Littleton got bit! Me and Lucy was walking the little ones to where they could get a good look down the cliff to the river. Amos was running to catch up, when he tripped and let out a holler. I ran back. He was crying loud and scared. I saw something flicking out of the corner of my eye. I started to poke the brush, when it slithered out, a long, mean-looking rattler, shaking its tail and hissing angry. I picked up a big rock and started moving away from where Amos was laying, all the while talking real loud to get the rattler's mind on me. Lucy tried pulling Amos away ever so slow, but the rattler caught on. It turned its head to follow Amos and started to curve back to strike. I began to stomp and holler loud as I could. Then I hurled the stone at it and missed! The hissing was something fierce. I grabbed a bigger stone and this time smashed it down on the head. The tail shook a couple of times, and then it was gone.

Lucy had torn open Amos's pant leg. The bite holes was just below his knee. I tied my belt on his thigh tight enough to try to stop the poison from moving up to his heart. He was white as a ghost and shaking. I cut an X through the bite and started sucking. I saw Pa do that once on Sam the field hand who was helping with our crop. "Just keep sucking and spitting till you got no more spit in you." So that's what I was doing, sucking and spitting, sucking and spitting.

Lucy left me with Amos and the little kids, and ran back to the wagons. Soon Mr. Littleton and Mr. Welch was out there with a litter. By this time Amos was passed out. They carried him back and took him to Mr. Fenster's wagon. I walked the children to the wagons. We all was examining the ground real careful.

Later

Tonight at supper Missus Henshaw said I probably saved Amos's life. Bekky was clapping real excited, "I was there! I was there!" Mr. Henshaw muttered, "Real hero," and Missus Henshaw looked at him hard.

August 11

Amos has got a bad fever. His leg is swollen up, and Mr. Littleton's real worried. When I was working with him today, he said Amos was all he got left. Missus Littleton died two years ago giving birth to a little girl who also died. Mr. Littleton's sister had been living with them, keeping house and taking care of Amos, but she didn't want to come on the trip. She's back in Missouri. Mr. Littleton wanted to make a new life, so that's why he and Amos is here.

"I promised Missus Littleton when she was dying I'd guard over Amos with my life," he said. "If he passes . . ." And then he couldn't say any more. Only time I seen Mr. Littleton choked up like that. Me and the boys had wondered where Missus Littleton was. Somebody said maybe she'd run off with someone else, but it didn't figure right, him being the nice man he is.

Mr. Littleton's been telling me more. Needs to keep talking I guess while we wait. Seems Missus Littleton used to read out loud at night when they were finished up with supper. All kinds of books. Maybe that's why he listens so close whenever Mr. Fenster reads. He says it's a pleasure hearing someone tell a story from a book. Can make you forget everything else going on.

August 12

Traveled a real long day, trying to find water for the animals. Tried several times to get down to the river, but the cliffs are just too high. In some spots, Mr. Littleton says, we're a thousand feet up from the river. Even when we get close, we can't always get down. Charlie, Jack, and me was helping scouting for places, but it was miles before we could get down to the bottoms. If it's hard on us seeing all that water, it must be driving the cattle crazy smelling it.

August 13

Mr. Littleton had some hard news today. Jacob Fenster come over while I was there mid-day. I heard him say if Amos was to live, his leg has got to come off. Mr. Littleton sat there, staring like he was seeing something way faraway. Mr. Fenster put his hands on Mr. Littleton's shoulders. "Hiram, you hear me?" Mr. Littleton nodded, and then Mr. Fenster nodded and said he'd bring the boy back.

I ran to get Missus Henshaw, and she told me to tell the Captain and to alert Missus Simpson and Missus Sedlow and tell them to bring some clean sheets and large kettles. By the time I got back to Mr. Littleton's wagon, there was a fire going with a kettle of water coming to a boil. Missus Henshaw had spread a blanket out with a pile of her best sheets cut in squares.

The Taler twins organized a group of men and boys to cut as much wormwood and sage stalks as they could find to keep the fires going. Mr. Henshaw went out with the fuel crew. Missus Cavendish warned Mr. Grouch not to say a word, just to keep stoking the fire.

Captain Osborne had a bottle of whisky and a piece of board sanded smooth. Mr. Fenster took charge. If it was anybody else, Mr. Littleton would be doing the operating, but not on Amos. Missus Sedlow took Mr. Littleton aside and poured him a cup of coffee. Captain Osborne put a shot of whisky into it and said, "The rest is for Amos. Now don't worry, Hiram, it'll be fine."

Mr. Fenster stuck a knife into the fire and then dipped it in a cup of whisky. Captain then poured some whisky into Amos and told him to bite down on the wood. Mr. Fenster wrapped Amos's leg above and below where he was going to cut. I was scared to look, and so I don't know about the first cut. Amos was moaning real loud. Captain kept saying, "Bite down, son! Bite down real hard!" Then suddenly there was no more moaning. When I looked around, Amos had passed out.

"Easier for him," Mr. Fenster said. Then he took up Mr. Littleton's saw and started to cut through the leg bone. Missus Henshaw was wiping Amos's face the whole time. So she saw everything. My knees started to buckle under me, so I left and went round the back of the wagon where Mr. Littleton was drinking his coffee. Missus Sedlow was holding his arm. I sat down on the ground and told him it was going just fine. He peered at me wanting to believe that, and nodded. The three of us sat through the afternoon. I don't think I want to be a doctor.

August 14

Amos is better! Mr. Littleton sat up with him all through the night, and this morning his fever was gone. Mr. Littleton's been telling Amos he's going to make him the best wooden leg in this great land, and better than all the crowned heads of Europe have ever seen.

August 15

Captain Osborne was smiling this morning at the council meeting before calling roll-out. He said we'd be coming up on Salmon Falls where we could set aside the bacon and get some of that pink fish "to satisfy these tired-out taste buds!" interrupted Mr. Grouch. He's been a bit pleasanter since Mr. Littleton adjusted his teeth, but he still never checks his tongue.

Heard the pounding and roar of the Salmon Falls well before we come on it. As we approached, it looked like hundreds of red cloths were flapping in the breeze. When we got closer, I walked up to get a better look. Charlie was already there. It was a sight to see. Red fish was hanging from dozens of lines, drying in the sun.

We were in a small village made up of about twenty Indian huts. Canoes lined the riverbank, and these drying lines were strung all over. Both the men and women of this village made it clear they wanted to trade.

Our men went through their supplies looking for any powder or balls, hooks or knives they could spare. The ladies unpacked pants and dresses, blouses and shirts, pieces of calico. The Indians were interested in almost anything we had to offer. All we wanted was salmon, and so it was a friendly exchange.

Charlie was complaining we still hadn't met any of the treacherous Indians the Talers had told about. Mr. Grouch overheard us. "Just be grateful we're not trading you!" and he poked his bony elbow into Charlie's back.

"Not a bad idea," Mr. Henshaw muttered as he passed. "You, too," he said, pointing at me. Those two really should be friends.

Later

Supped on fish, oily and tasty. Even Mr. Henshaw seemed pleased with the change in the fare.

August 17

I counted eight dead oxen and cows from companies that is ahead of us. We've been climbing up and down hills and ravines. It's hard to find good patches of grazing. And we seen too many pools of alkali water. Had to drive the animals hard to keep them from it. Yesterday we carried water up a 500-foot bluff to bring it to camp for drinking and cooking, and we was lucky. The Talers and six others had to drive the cattle nearly four miles before those poor creatures could get a drink.

August 18

Today I was scared. As scared as I've been at any of the bad river fordings since the Kaw. Captain Osborne stopped the company and said we was about to start walking along a narrow ridge that was going to last for about a mile. He said everyone had to be walking either in front of or behind the wagons. There was no room on the sides, for the ridge was about as wide as the wagons. Mr. Littleton come up and asked Mr. Henshaw to let me to guide his team, as he had to carry Amos.

The gorge on the left looked to be a thousand feet down to the bottom, Captain had said. And on the right, it was a sheer drop at least as far, straight down to the river. From up here the river looked to be only a few inches wide! I got to thinking, if Charlie was dizzy looking down into Devil's Gate, how's he going to do on this Devil's backbone?

He told me later his eyeballs ached from staring so hard straight in front of him. Never even saw the gorge or the river. Maybe that was the smart thing to do.

August 19

After we traveled a while this morning, Missus Henshaw said, "Out of the frying pan and into the fire." She was staring at the river below a steep bluff we had to go down. If the ridge was bad, the river looked worse. But the Captain said this was the best place to ford the Snake, and so we got ready.

We had to cross to one island and then a second before we could climb up the other bank of the river. I was none too happy, but the cattle were. There was plenty of grass on the islands, so they got their first good meal in days. Missus Simpson rode in Mr. Littleton's wagon, watching over Amos. So this time I stayed with the Henshaws.

Getting to the first island was easy. Then we had to

drive almost sideways to get to the second, but it weren't too bad. From there to the shore was a different kettle of fish. Mr. Fenster marked it out with his poles, and you could see the bottom was real uneven with some deep holes. The Talers swam across with ropes to guide us, and each wagon got hooked up with four or six yoke of oxen. The current was real swift, and you needed as much strength pulling the wagons as you could get. Mr. Henshaw's grease bucket got knocked off, and I think maybe a sack of flour from the Simpsons' wagon was ruined.

We was already on shore when I heard the hollering. Even with all the safeties in place, two wagons tipped over! It's lucky one wasn't the Littleton wagon, what with Amos lying in there. And a lucky thing there was enough men in the water to hang onto the toppled wagons, so only a chest, a mirror, and some clothing got swept away. These folks were lucky, is all I can say.

I'm waiting for a time when I don't think so much about a crossing.

August 21

Indians stole Mr. Pringle's horse last night. This morning they come and offered to sell it back. Puts me in mind of the story about Mr. Lovejoy. Mr. Henshaw and a couple of the other men was ready to shoot the Indians, but the Captain steered them away, and Mr. Pringle gave up his best knife in a trade for his own horse.

August 23

We're staying in camp, 'cause according to Missus Sedlow, if we don't stop for a wash-up, the weight of the dirt is going to drown us all on the next crossing. The boys went out to gather as much burn-ables as they could find. There's more trees here than we have seen in a long time. Some of the men, Mr. Henshaw included, smoked and played cards. Mr. Grouch was hanging over them, pointing out whenever someone threw the wrong card. The Captain, Mr. Hall, and Mr. Fenster spent time looking at maps. And Mr. Littleton had me doing a lot of the easy repair work, 'cause he was refining Amos's wooden leg, making it real special. He said he thought both the leg and Amos would be ready for each other by the time we got to Fort Boise.

We've been following the Boise River, and at campfire tonight I found out how it got named. This time Mr. Fenster told the story. Seems, back in 1833, Captain Bonneville come through here. He and his men was so excited to see all this green after what they'd been footing through, the Captain cried out, "*Les bois, les bois, voyez les bois!*" Me and Charlie started laughing, but Missus Cavendish told us to mind our manners. "That's French, boys. Time you had some real learning." Mr. Fenster translated: "The trees, the trees, look at the trees!" I guess it makes sense they'd be excited. But like I said to Charlie, "Heck, just 'cause you get excited don't mean you have to talk French!"

August 24

Mr. Littleton carried Amos out to the campfire tonight so he won't feel trapped having to stay so much of the time in the wagon. Everybody knew he was coming, and all the little ones, Amos's friends, was allowed to stay up late. The Taler twins was in high gear.

"What do you think, Micah?" asked Jeremiah, when we were all gathered by the fire. "What good is a wooden leg?"

Micah was struggling mightily to scratch a spot on his back he couldn't reach either from the bottom or the top. "A back scratcher! Will you lend me your leg when you get it, Amos?"

"What about it, children?" Jeremiah asked. "What else is it good for?"

"No musKEEEtows can ever itch you on your wooden leg!" Bekky piped up.

Lucy's little sister said, "And no ole rattlesnake can bite that leg again!"

Others chimed in:

"Make a great flagpole for the Fourth of July!"

"Beat a robber over the head if he breaks in during the night!"

"Lean on a barrel and use your leg for a ball bat!"

"Shove it in a grizzly's mouth when he roars, so he can't bite your head off?"

"Kick a ball harder than anyone else in the whole world!" hollered Amos.

And that made Mr. Littleton smile.

August 27

We're at Fort Boise and back near the Snake River. Amos is healing fast, but Mr. Littleton said he's not quite ready to strap on his new leg. Amos complains he wants to get up and start kicking at balls and stones. But his pa says it'll take a while before he learns to walk with his new leg. I'd want to get going, too, if it was me waiting on a new leg.

Later

We're getting close! At the Fort they're selling Oregon City flour. It's too dear to buy, Missus Henshaw says, but just thinking about how it come all the way from a city called OREGON is something.

August 28

Not too long after roll-out, we crossed the Snake River. Took about three hours. We emptied the wagons out, and I have to admit I agree with Mr. Henshaw's grumbling here. Almost all we do is load and unload these wagons. Anyways, we unloaded, cut poles, and layed them across the top of the beds, and then reloaded. The wagons were heavy and steady, and everything stayed dry raised up like that. We corralled soon after crossing. Captain says we'll be leaving the Snake here and heading for the Powder River bottoms.

August 29

Mr. and Missus Henshaw was arguing hard this morning when we got to a fork in the road. He wanted to take the

cutoff layed out by a Mr. Stephen Meek, who was pilot-
ing a company behind us. Captain Osborne says he heard
about this plan back at Fort Hall. Captain's a fair man and
gave the men Meek's account. By cutting west down the
Malheur River, Meek had said, and then across the plains,
the trail keeps you out of the Blue Mountains and brings
you to the Deschutes River, which you then take up to
the Columbia. In all, according to Meek, you save about
150 miles, maybe ten days. But the Captain was advising
against it. "No wagons have gone that route, and most
people say there's dried-up plains out there and not
much water. The heat will be something fierce, and the
grazing is likely to be poor."

Jacob Fenster said "Malheur" is French for "misfortune," and sometimes things are named for a good reason.
In the end most of the men voted to stay with the
Captain, but six said they were taking their families on
this shortcut. They decided to lay by and wait for the
company organizing out of Fort Boise to take the Meek
route. Mr. Henshaw would have been the seventh, but
Missus Henshaw said she trusted the Captain who had
got us this far. She'd rather walk the rest of the way, she
said, holding Bekky's hand, and rely on the kindness of
her neighbors, then leave the Captain. Mr. Henshaw was
so angry, I thought a blood vessel in his neck was going to

burst. He yelled at me for ten minutes straight about nothing at all. But we stayed with the company.

August 31

The road has been rough going in places, and I have been leading the team a fair bit. Mr. Henshaw's whupping them a lot, and when Missus Henshaw gets real upset, he goes back to the cattle. With the rotating of men working the cow column, he's not needed so much, but he goes anyways.

Later

Missus Henshaw says I'm a very lucky boy! I guess so. The Captain's real angry about the whole thing. Not at me, though. Every morning he's been saying, "Take the caps out of your firearms when you're storing them."

We had been walking in a stony, narrow streambed, with the wagons creaking and groaning with every step. Our wagon was behind the Bogarts'. I was up front on the left side, leading the team, when there was a sudden splash and a blinding flash of light. I fell back into the stream and smelled burning hair. It took me a minute to realize it was mine! I didn't see what happened, but on reconstructing, Captain said Joseph Bogart's rifle must have fallen off the back of his wagon when one of the rear wheels went up and over a rock. When the firearm hit the streambed, it went off.

The shot went through my new hat. Lucy said she'd make me another, but I said I wanted to keep this one. Since the crown stayed on and the shot just singed my hair, I'm taking it that it's my lucky hat.

Charlie says I'm the cat with nine lives. There's two down, and I don't want to chance any more.

Mr. Henshaw looked shaken. If he'd have been where he was supposed to be, I wouldn't have near got killed. But then him being taller, he might have got killed. No wonder he was pale.

September 2

The trail's been following the creek. Sometimes we're in the bed, sometimes up the side of the mountain. Today me and Charlie and Jake got to work with the men clearing the trail. Mr. Henshaw has two axes, and I was using the lighter one. We had to hack through thickets of scrubby cedars, alder, birch, and all kind of prickly briars.

My buckskin pants is a wonder. They got scratched bad, but none of it come through. My arms is a different story. Mr. Fenster fixed all of us up with a salve, which took the burning away.

At supper, Mr. Henshaw kept pointing at Missus Henshaw, saying it was her fault we weren't following the Meeks' road. "They's probably nearly at the Columbia by now!" She told me to take Bekky over to the Sedlows for half an hour, so I don't know what more got said.

September 3

We have a new member in the company! And Charlie's got a new cousin. Missus Welch has been riding with different folks since she lost her wagon to a cart. She's even been with us a few times, but lately Mr. Henshaw's in such a black state of mind, Missus Henshaw didn't think it was good for a lady who's carrying to be around that. Missus Welch was with the Simpsons the past few days. Just before we was supposed to stop for mid-day rest, Mr. Simpson pulled out his wagon. The Captain stopped the whole company 'cause Missus Cavendish announced it was time. Missus Cavendish knows about these things, and she went and delivered Charlie's aunt of a son! They're naming him Seth. Missus Simpson's making some permanent room in her wagon for the nursing mother. "No place for a baby in a cart," she told Mr. Simpson. He didn't put up no argument. I helped Charlie carry some of the Simpsons' things to his uncle's cart, so there'd be room for Missus Welch and the baby to lie down. Missus Henshaw had me bring over a quilt for the baby. His face is all red and scrunched up so tight, he looks a little like Mr. Perkins. I expect he won't be a grouch, though, not with Charlie as his cousin.

Preacher Turnbow did the christening right away. No point waiting four days to Sunday, Missus Sedlow said. "Who knows where we'll be in four days. Could be hanging off a mountainside." The Welches agreed. The ladies brought out the brandy and the men, the whisky. We drank milk. Missus Simpson had a cake she'd made a few days ago.

September 4

Amos got his leg strapped on! When we nooned, he tried it out. His face pinched up every time he put his weight on it, but he never let out a single holler. Mr. Fenster told him it will only get easier. "You're going to develop a callus and then a real strong muscle," he said. Amos kept on walking up and down, practicing for near two hours. I think he's trying to speed up getting that callus. Mr. Littleton carved him a cane to help him balance. It's got a buffalo head on it, and Mr. Littleton promised he'd teach me how to carve like that.

September 7

Told Charlie I think Missus Sedlow has got a crystal ball hidden in that trunk of hers. It's Sunday and we're on a mountain. About an hour after roll-out this morning, the road started winding up from the streambed along the mountainside. The trail was slanting so sharply, we stopped and let one wagon go at a time. Two big men sat on the upper side of the wagon to weigh it down. We lost a small box hanging off the downside, but it only had a broken knife and two cups. I think there were a few other mishaps like that, but nothing serious.

Amos walked the whole stretch!

September 8

Mr. Henshaw had me jumping into my pants extra fast this morning. Two of our six cows is missing. Seems we're not the only ones. The guards last night must have been napping, for at least twenty-five of the herd can't be found, including four horses. The grazing is in patches here, so you can see why they'd wander. But somebody should have been watching.

We finally found all but one cow belonging to Samuel Hall, and two horses. You'd think it was ours still missing, the way Mr. Henshaw was cussing. Anyways, we finally yoked up and headed out. The trail is stony and very uneven. We're headed up to a ridge overlooking the Grande Ronde Valley, which the Captain says is a good place to lay by. I expect it will be a long day.

Early afternoon

Malheur! But it's not the wagons on the Meek trail. It's us! It happened like this. I was leading the team and Charlie was walking with me. Mr. Henshaw was in the wagon fixing something he said was broke. We hit a rough patch coming down into the valley, and his revolver must have fallen off its hook. When he picked it up, it went off in his hand. We found him bleeding something awful. Charlie and I lifted him down onto the ground. I told Charlie to get Missus Henshaw, who was at the Sedlows' wagon, and then the Captain.

I folded a blanket under Mr. Henshaw's head. He stared up at me like he didn't know who I was. A little bit of blood was trickling out the side of his mouth. I told him I was going to get Mr. Fenster. I couldn't tell if he heard me or even knew what I was saying.

When I got back, Missus Henshaw and the Captain was already there. The rest of the company was gathering around. Lucy kept the young ones away. She told Bekky her pa was hurt bad, but it was better if Bekky stayed back and let Mr. Fenster do his work. Some of the ladies started boiling water and tearing up sheets.

Missus Henshaw was crying quietly, "I begged him, I begged him!" Captain Osborne took me aside and asked about the caps. I told him Mr. Henshaw paid the warning no mind. "Stubborn as a jack-ass," Captain muttered. I know he was thinking it was Mr. Henshaw's own fault. But maybe it's mine for not being more careful where the team walked. Or for sometimes wishing he was dead.

Later

Mr. Fenster did what he could, but the wound was too great, he said. It was only a matter of time, maybe an hour or two. He and Mr. Littleton wrapped Mr. Henshaw in blankets to keep him as warm as possible and lifted him

133

back into the wagon. Captain emptied the rifle that was still hanging there. "We've got to move on," he said. "The valley will be a good resting place for Asa. It's wide and peaceful." Missus Henshaw nodded, and climbed in to sit by her husband.

It was a miserable journey down into the valley. But the biggest misery was inside me, not on the trail, 'cause many's the day I had wished Mr. Henshaw dead.

"He's passed," Missus Henshaw said. But we kept rolling on. After we corralled, Captain, Mr. Sedlow, Mr. Fenster, and Mr. Simpson came over and took Mr. Henshaw out of the wagon, folded the blanket gently over his head and carried him off a few yards. "Almost got there, Asa. Pretty damned close." The Captain turned to Missus Henshaw. "It's cool here, and he'll be fine. We'll bury him in the morning." With that, they all left, except Mr. Fenster who hung back for a moment wanting to know if there was anything he could do. I had my arm around Bekky's shoulders. She was shivering. Missus Henshaw smiled slightly and shook her head. "We'll be fine, Jacob."

When we were alone, Missus Henshaw took a quick look at the dark form, and then steered me and Bekky to the other side of the wagon. "We're going on, Jedediah, like before. We have all lost family, and we are all going on." She sighed. "You'll have more chores, but I know you can do it." Then she said we all needed to get some sleep.

September 9

It was hard falling asleep last night. Part of me was feeling nothing, part of me was angry, and part of me was miserable. But Mr. Fenster woke me *after* roundup, so I guess I slept pretty deep.

In a short time everybody had gathered. They carried Mr. Henshaw to an open, grassy spot. Some of the men began to dig. Preacher Turnbow was there with his Bible, murmuring about the "Dearly Departed." I was standing in the back. I saw Missus Henshaw looking around for me, but I stayed behind. In my head I kept saying over and over, "He's not *my* dearly departed."

There was a light touch on my arm. Missus Cavendish was next to me. "He wasn't like a father to you, Jedediah, but he did take you in." She peered at me closely. "I didn't like him much, either, but if I can give him my coffin, you can pay him your respects."

I pushed my way through the group and took Bekky's hand as I slipped next to her. "Nearer, my God, to Thee, nearer to Thee!" Reverend Turnbow was starting the second verse:

Though like the wanderer, the sun gone down,
Darkness be over me, my rest a stone.
Yet in my dreams I'd be nearer, my God, to Thee.
Nearer, my God, to Thee, nearer to Thee!

A wanderer, his rest a stone. Suddenly my anger was gone. He wasn't like a father, but he had taken me in. I squeezed Bekky's hand.

Small cups of plum wine were passed out to all the grown-ups. Missus Cavendish handed me one. "I guess this means I'm going to have to survive this trip!" she said. "If I can't go under, I'm staying on top." And she clicked her cup against mine.

Later

It was a bright sun as we crossed the valley. Tall pines covered the mountainside. "We're finished with burning sage," Charlie said, pointing to all that wood. He was walking again with me. The cart was fairly easy for his uncle to handle, since his aunt and little Seth were still most days in the Simpsons' wagon.

We nooned at the upper end of the valley. We were still unyoking, when a group of Indians rode up and surrounded our camp. The women were on saddles with very high horns in front and back. Some of them had babies wrapped up in sacks with stiff boards. They looked like huge butterfly cocoons, hanging off the front horn of the saddle. Only thing you could see was these little round faces sticking out the top.

I told Charlie I thought that would be a great way to carry Seth. You could hang him up in the wagon, and Missus Welch could do whatever she wanted. "And I bet the rocking of the wagon would put him to sleep."

Charlie thought it was a great idea. "End some of that infernal racket Lucy's been complaining about," he said. She's been helping out at the Simpsons. Seems Seth has been a little colick-y, and howling about it. I'm real glad he hasn't been staying with us.

The Indians stayed to trade. According to the Captain, they're Cayuse and maybe some Nez Percé who have been learning some farming up by the Whitman Mission and from the other missionary, Mr. Spalding. They brought corn and pumpkins, potatoes and peas, and of course fish. We traded clothes, cloths, and tools. They also wanted to swap horses for our cows. The Taler twins and Mr. Pringle were glad for the trade, since they lost horses the other day. We all ate together in a big feast laid out on oil cloths. The Indians had this root they call camas. Abigail Appleton says it's a kind of lily. I said, "Looks to me like a small onion with a pulled-out end." She said, "Same family." Ned smiled real wide, like he was proud she knew things like that. I'm never going to look at anyone mushy like that, even if maybe I do get married.

Anyways, this camas root is real sweet. They had it raw and also ground up and boiled in patties. Can't decide which I like better. A couple of Indian boys our age came over to where Jack, Charlie, and me were sitting. They was as curious about us as we was about them. One of them held out a camas root. Jack pulled out a nail from his pocket. The Indian boy nodded. "Looks like we can do our own trading," Jack said. We went off with them, and pretty soon we had a brisk exchange going of nails and any scraps of metal for roots. We ~~was~~ were as busy as the grown-ups. I think we got the best deal. I got enough camas to last me a week.

I'm still having trouble with the plurals. Lucy corrects me sometimes, but I forget when I'm writing things down. Maybe it's 'cause I'm writing a lot in the dark.

September 10

Four families said they was real low on supplies, and so they went north to the Whitman Mission. Two of the Cayuse offered to be their guides. At the council meeting this morning, Captain said we will all meet up again at the Umatilla River.

For the second time on this journey, I was the subject of a council meeting! This time, Captain said, seeing as I was the male in the Henshaw wagon, and seeing as I had been attending most of the meetings, if I had something I wanted to say, they'd all be pleased to hear it. Can't think of anything I could say. All I have is questions, but I didn't say that.

Later

We're in the Blue Mountains. We double-teamed several times, 'cause the climb was so steep. After four or five miles, we came down off a ridge and crossed the Grande Ronde River. Good grass on the bottoms, and we camped here. Mr. Littleton and Mr. Fenster are talking to me like I was not just a boy, but more like one of them. "What do you think, Jedediah, about . . . ," and "Supposing, Jedediah, we take . . ." Makes me nervous I won't give them the right answer, but they don't seem to be waiting on me to say anything. More like including me in the plans. It's making Charlie look at me a little funny, but I can't help that.

Evening

Mr. Fenster came over and supped with us. Some of the men had killed a deer, and we were dining richly. I contributed a few camas, which Missus Henshaw roasted. When we finished and was sitting back, digesting, as Pa used to say, she asked me about the things Mr. Henshaw had been repairing. I had forgotten all about them. She said she wondered if Mr. Littleton could help me with them.

Mr. Fenster sat smoking his pipe, listening. Then he says he has this plan he's been meaning to talk to her about. He wants to give the Welches his wagon, 'cause he, Mr. Fenster, doesn't have a wife or a baby, and if Missus Henshaw would like, he'd be pleased to help work our wagon. He has his own tent, and with his added team, he said, he thought it would be a lot easier on the trail.

Missus Henshaw was looking a little interested, I thought. I mean, wasn't I doing all right? I think Mr. Fenster must have heard my thinking, 'cause he said real quick, "Of course, Jedediah here's been handling things real well, but I thought this way I could help out the Welches and get some good cooking, which I sorely crave." That settled it.

Anyways, that's how I come to be living with Mr. Fenster again.

September 11

Lucy is right. She was saying when we nooned that this Oregon was a grand and beautiful country. We've been up and down deep ravines, across open plains and through thick groves of trees. We've had to stop three times to clear the trail. I'm using Mr. Henshaw's big ax, 'cause Mr. Fenster has his own. So I guess that's all right. Takes some careful measuring, 'cause all the wagons have to be able to clear the tree stumps. And of course you've got to be careful where you chop, so nothing falls on any of the wagons. Haven't seen this many trees since we left the States.

Captain says we've crossed the main ridge of the Blue Mountains. He pointed to Mount Hood far in the distance. We're looking at one hundred and fifty miles away, he said! The mountain's snowy top looks like it's melting up into the sky. This morning Mr. Hall said at the council meeting that Mount Hood's just south of The Dalles. That means right now we're looking at almost the end of the journey!

September 13

Washing, cleaning, fixing. That was the whole day until late in the afternoon. That's when Mr. Littleton gave me my first carving lesson. First thing he said was, I had to respect the knives. "You'll do sloppy work, or you'll cut yourself. Maybe both, and it'll be because you don't respect the knives." He showed me how he worked the edge on a sharpening stone, and then stropped the knives on a piece of rawhide. I wanted to start carving, but he kept working the blades. At last he gave me a block of wood, and had me practicing certain cuts. I wasn't real sure what he meant about respecting, but after two hours struggling with that block, I sure respect *him* for what he can do with these knives.

Whenever I got discouraged, he showed me how these cuts I was working on was part of the buffalo head on Amos's cane. I made well over a hundred cuts on the block. He seemed pleased with at least the last five. Said I had to keep on practicing. We sharpened up the knife Pa gave me, so I can practice whenever I get a chance. I think it'll be a long while before I can carve a buffalo head.

Later

The group that went to the Whitman Mission rejoined up with us.

September 15

For two days we've followed the river, sometimes along the banks, other time up on the bluffs. The Indians are trading smoked fish as well as venison and vegetables. Seems they most want our clothing. We had a shared supper last night, with the food we've all bartered for. "I'm eating well," Mr. Grouch snorted, as he built a pile of fish bones on the side of his plate. "But I may soon be half neked in my drawers!" I nearly choked on a bone. Lucy whispered she didn't much fancy seeing Mr. Perkins in his drawers, but he may be right. She's got her one dress left, she said, and an overblouse and jacket. Missus Henshaw has been parceling out bits of Mr. Henshaw's clothes in trade. "There's not much left, but I still have my drawers," I said.

"She don't fancy seeing you in your drawers, either!" Charlie laughed until the tears was running down his face.

September 16

Captain said at the council meeting we'd reach the Columbia River in two or three days. When he finished assigning the guards for tonight's rotation, I said something. I was surprised to hear myself talking, but it happened just like that. "I want to be on the roster for guard duty," I said. Everybody looked at me. Some of them thought I was crazy, 'cause they don't want the rotation. Mr. Bogart said I was too young. "Amen," said Preacher Turnbow. It was Ned Appleton who spoke up for me. "You remember it was Jedediah Barstow who alerted us to that white Indian raid. And though it wasn't guard duty, Jedediah Barstow was out there helping turn the buffalo from us." The Captain added that if Missus Henshaw was satisfied with me helping to run her wagon — he looked at Mr. Fenster, who nodded — then I was competent enough to stand guard. But he said it wouldn't be tonight. It'll be in the rotation order where Mr. Henshaw used to be. Which, I guess, is fittin', since that's when I did it before.

September 18

We're nooning, and the Columbia River is four miles away! Everybody is excited, not just me. I think the teams are walking lighter. Charlie said that was ridiculous. They're exhausted, he said, and if we're not careful, our excitement might kill them off. I told him he was sounding like Mr. Grouch.

Later

There's the river! Even Mr. Grouch is staring without saying a word. Jack finally broke the silence. He flung his hat up. "Hooray for Oregon!" he hollered. "Amen!" the Reverend boomed. Amos let the little kids beat on his leg like a drum. "O-REE-GON! O-REE-GON!"

September 19

We passed a number of Indian villages, and we traded for smoked fish. I think near everybody traded for some. It'll be fish for supper the next few days.

September 20

We've been following along the Columbia, mostly on the sandy plains away from the narrow strip of bottom. We're all getting tired of walking. Charlie said he was so looking forward to being on a wooden floor, he'd even be happy to scrub one. I told him not to talk so loud. His aunt might hear.

At the council meeting this morning, Captain Osborne said we'll soon be crossing John Days River and then the Deschutes River. From there we're almost to The Dalles. Everybody was murmuring about The Dalles, 'cause after The Dalles we've got easy passage to our new home. But I'm not thinking about The Dalles. I'm thinking about those other rivers that come first. When's it going to stop, this feeling? It's like a shiver that moves up from my toes to my stomach. I can't tell Charlie about it. Nobody.

Later

When I brought Bekky over to the Sedlows' for the mid-day class, Lucy was all excited about being almost there. Said it gave her a special energy she was spreading over the children. In fact, she was going to take them for a walk, "to keep all their joints greased." She laughed. "I'm sounding like Mr. Littleton working on an axle." I wasn't in a laughing mood. I started to turn away when she said, "Why don't you come with us?" I didn't feel like talking to Mr. Littleton, or sitting with Missus Henshaw and Mr. Fenster, or seeing Charlie and Jack when I was feeling like this. So I went. Me and the little children. That's fittin'.

We walked for a while, and then Lucy asked me what was I pondering so serious on. I'd been seeing the Kaw River over and over in my head, and I blurted out, "I hate big river crossings!" She got real quiet. Sometimes I wish I could button up my mouth.

I thought she'd poke me and tell me not to be such a fraidy-cat. But she didn't. She said, "I was looking at Amos walking with his new leg, and I was thinking about that terrible day. How you were jumping around trying to get that ole rattler to turn to you."

"First time I ever been so close to one of them killers," I said. "They are something to be feared."

"That's my question," she said. "Do you think you have to be really afraid before you can be really brave?"

We walked on, not talking, and then Lucy called to the little ones and we headed back.

September 21

We're above the John Day. Real steep climb up a bluff. Captain had us corral here. Tomorrow we'll make the descent and crossing. The stream pours over the rocks at a fierce speed, but the crossing's only about ten yards. That's tomorrow. Tonight I'm on guard duty!

September 22

My hand was too shak-y last night to write down what happened. I went out to where the Captain sent me at about eight o'clock. We had finished a fine fish dinner, and Missus Henshaw told me to go on. She and Bekky would wash up. When I took Mr. Henshaw's rifle, she said I could just holler for help if I needed it. But I told her I'd used Pa's shotgun lots of times, so she shouldn't worry. It wasn't really lots of times, maybe six, but that's not real lying, it's exaggerating.

Anyways, I was sitting out at my post, smelling on the breeze all that tasty fish everybody had been frying up. Closed my eyes, not sleeping, just enjoying the aroma. That's what Pa said whenever Mama made something real tasty. Just enjoying the aroma.

I think I felt it before I saw it. I know I heard it before

148

I saw it. A thick, heavy, padded thud, regular, like someone or something walking fast. I grabbed the rifle and
stood up. A huge block of darkness rose up. The only
thing I could make out was the teeth! It was making a
deep, low sound, and then I realized so was I. It lumbered
close enough for me to smell and feel the heat pouring
out of it. There wasn't time to aim and shoot. I started
swinging the rifle like it was one of Mr. Fenster's poles. I
don't know how long I was swinging. I heard my shirt
tear, and felt a hot streak on my arm. I kept on swinging.
At last it fell back, turned, and ran off. I must have stood
there shaking for a couple of minutes before I set up hollering, "BEAR! BEAR! BEAR!" until I was hoarse.

Men came running up from every part of the corral. I
heard someone yell "GRIZZLY!" And then, "Fish! It's the
damn fish they're after!"

Mr. Hall was talking to the Captain. "I heard about
some Indians up north burying caches of fish when they
go on an expedition, so they'd have something on the re-
turn trip," he said. "And now I remember hearing they
burn the grass on top of where they bury the fish to
throw off the scent. These critters have powerful noses."

"And sensitive ones," the Captain added. Then he
turned to me and said I'd probably hit the bear on its nose
in all my swinging, and it decided this dinner wasn't
worth the fight. "They are fattening up for winter, and

salmon is one of their favorite dishes. But they still got time left. Might have been angrier a couple of weeks from now."

Charlie was staring me and the cut on my arm, and then at the tracks. "Look at those claw marks! You are something," he said, "battling off a grizzly!" He put his foot in a paw print. That was almost the scariest thing of all — his boot only filled maybe two-thirds of the print! He kept repeating, "You are something. You kept on swinging. Probably would have killed you if you'd run. But you didn't. You kept on swinging."

Later on when I couldn't sleep, I was thinking about what Lucy said. Wonder if she's right.

Today everybody was talking about last night's grizzly attack and asking me questions. So many questions, I didn't think too much about the crossing. Anyways, it was short.

September 24

The Deschutes River is ten times the width of the John Day, and with a violent current. There's a series of falls, dropping maybe twenty feet just before it pours into the Columbia. At the council meeting Mr. Fenster said

"Deschutes" means "falls." Mr. Grouch looked at him and said, "If I'd have known about all this French, I would've stayed home!" Captain's used to this by now, and just kept on talking. Although some companies have forded higher up, he said we'd ferry. And he and Mr. Hall engaged several Indians to pilot us over in their canoes.

I was remembering Mr. Henshaw's complaining as we unloaded everything. This time, though, I wasn't complaining. I figure these Indians know the rivers real well, so I'm happy to be putting everything in their canoes.

Took about three hours, but nobody lost a thing. Just got a little wet.

September 25

I voted this morning for the first time at a council meeting. "We're a long day away from The Dalles," Captain said. "It's the end of the wagon route . . ." But before another word got said, Mr. Grouch pointed at Mr. Fenster and said he didn't want to know the meaning of "Dalles," 'cause he was sure *he* planned on telling us. Mr. Fenster said nothing. I'm not sure I want to know, either.

Anyways, whatever it means, we're going to start down the Columbia from a site above The Dalles. That was my vote. Mr. Hall and some of the men thought we should go straight to The Dalles 'cause there's pilots taking you down. Problem with that, said the Captain, was they're charging fifty to a hundred dollars a wagon. I know Missus Henshaw don't have that. Somebody said we'd have to be selling stock to meet the fare. And I know Missus Henshaw is hanging on real tight to her cattle. So when it come time to vote, I voted for upstream. This was our biggest split ever. Half the company is going with Mr. Hall to The Dalles. The rest of us is sticking with the Captain.

Said good-bye to the Taler twins and to Ned and Abigail Appleton. Mr. Grouch went with them, too. He said so long as he didn't know what Dalles meant, he was going to chance it. Missus Cavendish told him he was a fool. I think she's actually going to miss poking her finger at him.

September 26

We've started building rafts. There's a lot of timber around the river, and Charlie, Jack, and me have been out foraging. We've got three teams gathering up materials, and Mr. Littleton's supervising the building. A small group of wagons in another company arrived this morning. We're all working together on the rafts. In four or five days, Captain says, we'll be riding the river.

October 1

We started out with eight and a half on our raft. I'm counting little Seth Welch as a half, 'cause that's really all he is. It was a clear, sunny day. Mr. Fenster was poling in front and Mr. Welch in the back. Charlie and me each was stationed at the sides with poles to push off of any big rocks we might come near. Missus Henshaw, Bekky, and Missus Welch was with us, and Lucy was holding the baby. Since she'd been helping so much with little Seth these past weeks, her folks said she could come with us.

The river was smooth, and I was feeling pretty good after saving everybody from the grizzly. We were going along just fine. Lucy said the rocking of the raft had put Seth to sleep. There was a kind of ease, knowing our wagon days was over, and in a few more days we'd be at Oregon City and heading down to the Willamette Valley. We still had The Dalles to pass through, but somehow I knew that was going to be fine.

Then I started noticing little waves building up. All of a sudden we were flying down the river on a racing current! Ahead and off to the left, patches of water whirled in circles, making funnels that dragged down anything caught in them. Some tree branches floating down the river cracked like rifle shots as they were sucked down into one of the funnels.

We kept picking up more speed. The raft downriver from us must have been caught by underwater reeds and tree roots you couldn't see. It was bobbing in the river, but not moving. Both Mr. Fenster and Mr. Welch was working something fierce to push past it. The raft was from the other company, and was piled high with their belongings. Two men were working it. One was trying to free his pole from a tangle of roots. The other was facing us, wide-eyed, braced to push us off if we got close.

We missed them by less than a foot, but the maneuvering caused us to rock so violently, Bekky fell back and into the water. Lucy reached for her, and Seth dropped out of her lap into the river. Suddenly all three of them were caught up in swirling waters. Missus Welch's screams were drowned out by the roar of the current.

Even as I write this I can't believe what happened next. All I know is I dove into that blackness. Seth was dropping down like a small bundle. I swam under him and brought him up to the surface. We were both coughing up water. I could see Lucy off to my right, hanging on to Bekky with one hand and an overhanging tree branch with the other. Our raft had beached downstream about a hundred yards. I fought across the current and reached Lucy and Bekky. Seth was under my arm. I pulled myself along the branches till I could feel the ground under my feet. I left Seth up on shore and went back to pull Lucy and Bekky in. We dragged ourselves up the low bluff and lay there breathing hard.

That's how the others found us. We stayed there a long while, Missus Welch rocking Seth, and Missus Henshaw, Bekky. Mr. Fenster was plugging his pipe, and he and Mr. Welch were talking about farming. Lucy was sitting next to me, looking at the turns in the river. I looked around at us. Any stranger coming upon our group would think we were a couple of families. I guess we are.

October 2

In days we'll be at Oregon City. I'm going to be staying with Missus Henshaw, helping her with things. After yesterday, I know that everything's going to work out somehow. I'm going to get to where Pa and Mama wanted to be. I just wish I could tell them that, and that I know why they wanted to come out here to Oregon. And that I'm glad they wanted to make the trip.

So today I'm ending Mama's journal. It's a fitting end,

and I tell it so whoever reads this story in the years to come will know that Jedediah Barstow, son of Josiah and Sarah Barstow, brother of Sally Martha Barstow, is going to be living in the Willamette Valley, in the Territory of Oregon, just like his family planned.

Epilogue

~~❧~~

Jedediah Barstow and his friends did reach the Willamette Valley, including Missus Cavendish, who lived to the age of ninety-three, with a new coffin ready and waiting. Most everyone in Jed's company wintered over in Oregon City before heading down the next spring to the valley.

Every misfortune anticipated by Captain Osborne about the Malheur River route occurred. This, however, is the only grim news to report. Captain Osborne later wrote a guide book that remained popular until covered wagon traffic ceased.

Before departing for the Willamette Valley, Sarah Henshaw and Jacob Fenster became Mr. and Missus Fenster. Present at the ceremony were Jedediah and Bekky, Amos and Mr. Littleton, the Sedlows, Simpsons, Missus Cavendish, and Jasper Perkins. Amos, wearing a pair of long pants, walked with Bekky to the front of the judge's bench. The Taler twins, unable to attend, sent a written story in their place.

After three years in the valley, the Fensters moved back to Oregon City where Jacob became a judge in the new court system. The job permitted him to share his vast knowledge with those compelled to listen. When Oregon became the thirty-third state in 1859, Judge Fenster continued to serve with distinction in the court system until his death.

Missus Fenster was equally busy. With Missus Sedlow, she opened a day school for young girls. Enrollment was so brisk, additional instructors were sought. Lucy Sedlow, having completed her schooling, was one of the first to be hired.

Jedediah returned with the Fensters to Oregon City. Having tasted the pleasures of writing, he was now determined to be a man of pens, not plows. His first job was to describe, in words sufficiently compelling to draw customers, the opening of a lumber yard in Oregon City. One afternoon, having detailed the virtues of a new cobbler's shop, he decided to call a halt to these fictions.

That weekend he met with Charlie Smothers and Jack Simpson, who were in town at the market. They discovered none was happy in his work. Jed announced he wanted to be a writer. Charlie said he wanted to be a businessman. And Jack declared he liked selling at the market, and thought he was a salesman, not a farmer.

And so the three pooled their resources and started a

newspaper for the scattered farm families in the valley. Jedediah wrote, Charlie organized the office, and Jack sold subscriptions. Soon the weekly was sold in Oregon City as well. Six months later it became one of the first daily papers on the Pacific coast.

Jedediah wrote a series of articles about the continuing friendships of early Oregon emigrants. In one, he told of a Jasper Perkins who had tea with a Missus Cavendish once a week for twenty-one years until he passed on. According to later reports, Missus Cavendish never again found someone whose chest she so enjoyed poking.

We cannot report that Jedediah won a Pulitzer prize for his news writing, for he was eighty-five years old when the prizes were first awarded. He was, however, a very happy man. He and Lucy Sedlow, now Barstow, had four children who, with the blessings of their parents, grew up to do what their hearts told them. The best prize any person could have, Jedediah always said, was good work and a good family.

Life in America
in 1845

Historical Note

In the late 1830s and early 1840s, the name "Oregon" became synonymous with hope. The economic depression of 1837 forced thousands out of jobs, farms, and homes. Banks closed. Disease struck many communities, and hundreds died. Reports of Oregon's rich farm land and mild climate seemed to offer a chance for a new life.

And so thousands crossed the continent from east to west in search of a new beginning. Although there are no exact records, it is estimated that between 1841 and 1866 at least 350,000 people went west. Much of what we know about the westward trek comes from more than 800 published diaries and journals of emigrants.

Most people traveled by covered wagon. Some hoped to start new farms, some to escape from religious persecution. Others went in search of gold and silver. They traveled to today's states of California, Montana, Colorado, Nevada, Utah, and Oregon. Although there were several routes, including the California and Santa Fe Trails, the phrase the "Oregon Trail" is often used for all westward travel.

The actual Oregon Trail was the longest of the overland routes, some 2,000 miles from a "jumping off" point on the Missouri River — the towns of Independence, St. Joseph, and Council Bluffs — to the Willamette Valley in Oregon Territory. Families built or bought covered wagons, and carefully selected what to take. One important decision was choosing oxen, horses, or mules to pull the wagons. Oxen, slowest but most dependable, were most often selected.

At the jumping-off towns emigrants waited for the spring rains to end, the mud to dry, the prairie grass to grow high enough to feed the cattle, and then they pulled out. Timing was crucial: too early, and the grass wouldn't be sufficiently abundant; too late, and you might be trapped in the mountains in heavy snowfall.

Early in the journey, emigrants crossed into Indian territory, and for the first time saw exotic animals like buffalo, antelope, and prairie dogs. They trekked across wide grasslands and slowly ascended and crossed the South Pass of the Rocky Mountains.

Both the Americans and the British had western outposts. Each encouraged settlers from their nation to stake claims in the territories. In 1836, Dr. Marcus Whitman and his wife Narcissa, led a small party to Oregon. Their covered wagon was the first to travel west of Fort Hall. Dr. Whitman returned east to encourage more settlers. In 1843, he led a thousand people west. His urgent appeal for settlers is often credited with "saving" Oregon for the United States. In 1846, America and Britain agreed to the boundary that today separates Canada from the state of Washington.

During the early decades of travel, encounters between emigrants and Indians were largely peaceful. They exchanged information, traded, endured occasional thefts and misunderstandings, but generally went their separate ways. In the 1850s and 1860s when travelers began to settle in Indian territory, serious hostilities began.

From today's vantage point, traveling west in a covered wagon seems like a grand adventure. It was indeed, particularly for young people who didn't have the worries and responsibilities of their parents. But even for children, there were fearful times: fierce rainstorms with thunderous bolts of lightning; earthshaking buffalo stampedes; fevers with no name; and deaths from drowning, disease, and accidents.

News of such troubles deterred some from beginning the journey. Others turned back after traveling partway. But thousands continued west. Before 1849, there were no well-stocked trading posts until travelers reached Fort Laramie. Settlers had to bring everything they needed. In addition to food, clothing, tools, and other supplies, they also carried herbs and medicinal remedies. Wagons, clothing, shoes, and equipment were repaired over and over until they finally wore out.

Traveling the Oregon Trail involved hard work. Some days wagons were unloaded and reloaded half a dozen times to cross streams and rivers. Some crossings were easy, some treacherous. Axles and wheels bent and broke so often, every wagon train needed a blacksmith and carpenter. Women had a particularly challenging time cooking meals with little firewood, and often in wind, sand, and rainstorms. Yet for birthdays, weddings, and Fourth of July celebrations, they created feasts with supplies stashed away for just such occasions.

As tens of thousands of wagons rolled west, more trading posts opened. Bridges spanned rivers, and ferry services were established. Stagecoaches eventually replaced wagons, cutting the six-month trip in half. With the completion of the transcontinental railroad in 1869, cross-country travel by covered wagon was virtually at an end.

But the magic in the words "Oregon Trail" continues to conjure up pictures of covered wagons and sturdy pioneers. The very idea of the Oregon Trail seems to stand for the American genius for adventure. As well it should.

Pioneers heading west move out of Independence, Missouri, in a covered wagon train.

Upon reaching Fort Laramie, in Wyoming, travelers had completed one-third of the journey along the Oregon Trail. Built in 1834 as a fur-trading post, the fort stands as the gateway to the Rocky Mountains, where Native Americans, white fur trappers, and pioneers could trade and do business together.

Tired pioneers stop to take a break from the daily trials of traveling by wagon train.

Fording rivers and traveling through mountains were particularly hazardous challenges along the Oregon Trail. The covered wagons tended to tip and break easily in the narrow and uneven mountain passes, and the oxen pulling the wagons could lose their footing and fall, bringing the wagons down with them. Wagons could also tip or fall apart during river crossings, and passengers might fall out and be washed away.

The Rocky Mountains marked the final and most difficult leg of the Oregon Trail. Pioneers had to navigate narrow and bumpy passages through the mountains, and they had to be very careful about their timing. For to become caught in the mountains in winter, once snow began to fall, could be disastrous.

Oregon City was the first capital of Oregon. Built next to a narrow point in the Willamette River, Oregon City was a natural center for commerce. There, Native Americans and whites came together to trade. By 1845 Oregon City had more than five hundred residents, a number of tradespeople, seventy-five houses, two churches, two saloons, and their first daily newspaper.

About the Author

As a young person, Ellen Levine's favorite books were about pioneers and covered wagons. She always thought the adventure of traveling through unsettled territory and making everything you needed for the journey must have been a fascinating experience. Although she has traveled West, and on parts of the Oregon Trail, it was by car, plane, and train. But she has carved wooden spoons and a breadbowl, and made a bellows for a woodstove — all of which she says have offered her a small taste of the self-sufficient life.

Ellen Levine is the award-winning author of many acclaimed books, both fiction and nonfiction. Her book *Freedom's Children: Young Civil Rights Activists Tell Their Own Stories* won the Jane Addams book award and was named one of ALA Best Books for Young Adults, an NCSS Notable Children's Book, and one of the Ten Best Children's Books of the Year by the *New York Times*. *A Fence Away From Freedom: Japanese Americans and World War II* won the Carter G. Woodson Award and the *Parenting*

Reading Magic Award. Her most recent book, *Darkness Over Denmark: The Danish Resistance and the Rescue of the Jews*, won the SCBWI Golden Kite Award and the Jane Addams honor book award, was named one of ALA Best Books for Young Adults, and was a National Jewish Book Award finalist. Among her many Scholastic books are *If You Traveled West in a Covered Wagon; The Tree That Would Not Die; If Your Name Was Changed at Ellis Island; I Hate English!;* and *If You Lived at the Time of Martin Luther King.* Ms. Levine divides her time between New York City and Salem, New York.

In memory of my sister Dori Brenner, who would have loved to have made this journey, so long as she could have had a hot bath at the end of every day.

Acknowledgments

I am truly grateful for the support of my writers group, and am particularly indebted to Norma Fox Mazer, Harry Mazer, and Sandra Jordan. I also want to thank Dr. George Kivowitz and Peter Koedt — it's wonderful having friends who know about false teeth and grizzly bears. I am also most grateful to my editor, Beth Levine, who read and edited the manuscript with both a sensitive eye and a sure hand.

Grateful acknowledgment is made for permission to reprint the following:

Cover Portrait: Hulton/Archives.
Cover Background: The Granger Collection, New York.

Page 165 (top): Wagon train moves out of Independence, Missouri, Oregon Historical Society, Negative no. OrHi 5224 #838.
Page 165 (bottom): Fort Laramie, Walters Art Gallery.
Page 166: Taking a break from the Trail, Denver Public Library, Western History Department.
Page 167 (top): Fording the river, Western History Collections, University of Oklahoma Libraries.
Page 167 (bottom): Overturned wagon, Oregon Historical Society, Negative no. CN 023973 #0767Z001.
Page 168 (top): Crossing the Rocky Mountains, Engraving of a Frances Palmer painting, 1866, Courtesy of the Library of Congress.
Page 168 (bottom): Oregon City, 1845, Sketch by Henry Warre, Courtesy of the Oregon Historical Society, Negative no. OrHi 791 #838.

Foldout Map by Bryn Bernard.

Other books about the Journey Westward from
Dear America and My Name Is America

Across the Wide and Lonesome Prairie
The Oregon Trail Diary of Hattie Campbell
by Kristiana Gregory

West to a Land of Plenty
The Diary of Teresa Angelino Viscardi
by Jim Murphy

The Great Railroad Race
The Diary of Libby West
by Kristiana Gregory

Seeds of Hope
The Gold Rush Diary of Susanna Fairchild
by Kristiana Gregory

The Journal of Sean Sullivan
A Transcontinental Railroad Worker
by William Durbin

The Journal of Augustus Pelletier
The Lewis & Clark Expedition
by Kathryn Lasky

The Journal of Douglas Allen Deeds
The Donner Party Expedition
by Rodman Philbrick

While the events described and some of the characters in this book may be
based on actual historical events and real people, Jedediah Barstow is
a fictional character, created by the author, and his journal and its
epilogue are works of fiction.

The display type was set in Elli.
The text type was set in Berling Roman.
Book design by Elizabeth B. Parisi.
Photo research by Dwayne Howard.

ISBN 0-439-62523-8

3 4 5 6 7 8 9 10   23   12 11 10 09 08 07 06